Keepers of the Secret Code

by K J Williams and Teresa R. Kemp

ISBN 978-1-7358306-8-1 (hardcover)
ISBN 978-1-7358306-7-4 (paperback)

Doodle and Peck Publishing
413 Cedarburg Ct
Yukon, OK 73099
405.354.7422

www.doodleandpeck.com

Temporary cataloging topics: Underground Railroad, secret quilt codes, slavery, plantations, South Carolina, middle grade novel, African American history

Library of Congress Control Number: 2021944324

"For my mother who has sewn over 1,000 quilts for orphaned African babies, and who introduced me to this amazing piece of history."

KJ WILLIAMS

"Dedicated to all the young Peters and Elizas that will read our book and grow up to be abolitionists. May all of them continue working on the modern, secret Underground Railroad.
My unending gratitude to the five generations of my ancestors—for their faith, love of mankind, dedication, and bravery. They safeguarded the Underground Railroad secret quilt codes and passed down our legacy to successive generations until it could finally be proven true."

TERESA R. KEMP

Chapter 1

From the time I was knee high, I had nightmares of being forced to pick cotton. I could feel Overseer's wolf eyes watching, always on me. I didn't know why, but I sensed his hunger to break my spirit by working me hard in the fields. As a young'un playing 'round the big house, I'd forget he was there. I'd seen five year olds faint dead away from working "cain't see to cain't see" in the plantation's tobacco and cotton fields. If'n I survived the suffocating Carolina sun, I'd likely feel the whip on my back 'cause I knew I'd never be able to pick one hundred pounds a day; Overseer's quota.

At six years old, I felt safer when Master made me the fetch-and-carry boy. My daily chores was filling the wood boxes in all the rooms of the big house, pulling weeds in the vegetable garden and taking care of the horses, including shoveling out the stalls. I milked Bessie and Mort and helped out at mealtime, 'long with whatever else I was told to do. But lately, I felt jumpy. I wanted to do something different. Take on important, bigger chores. Be respected like Papa, who was Dover Hall's blacksmith or Sam the plantation's carpenter. But when you is an eleven year old enslaved boy, you don't get to choose anything 'bout your life.

At daybreak, like every day, I was fetching and carrying. Papa was splitting wood on the stump, as fast as I could pile it up. "Now, Peter, don't be draggin' your feet so you can watch the sunrise. God sho' do paint them pretty in South Carolina, but you gotta get that wood to the cookhouse." The sunrise reminded me of Mama's indigo and yellow quilts. Scout, a wolf-sized, mangy mutt trotted beside me. He was known 'round as the Farrow's family dog, to me he was more like the brother I never had. Many nights, I told him my feelings as we slept on the floor in our cabin. Most days he was Papa's shadow and hung 'round the blacksmith shed. But today when I picked up the chopped wood, he jumped right up and followed me.

I was restless, like a hunting dog that was straining at his chain. When I was twelve, would anything be different? Would I be the plantation's errand boy forever? Even though Mama and Papa called me a man child I was ready to take on man's work. I weren't as tall as Papa but I towered over Mama. Since I was skinny as a stick, some called me chicken legs. But I could lift more than most, 'cause of all my toting and carrying all over the place. I was ready to do something different, learn something new.

I figured my antsy was 'cause Em told me her Daddy, Massa, was thinking 'bout putting me to work with Dover's carpenter, Sam. I wanted it so bad. He was a lanky, dark skinned fellow who lived in the slave quarter behind our clapboard cabin. He never talked much but one day he told me 'bout being kidnapped and carried on a ship from Calabar, Africa just like Mama and Papa. I loved hanging 'round him. He smelled of fresh cut wood and was sprinkled in wood shavings. He was an easygoing fellow always whistling and smiling while he worked.

I trudged past the cotton fields. My heart hurt for my kinsmen, burlap sacks slung over their shoulders picking cotton as fast as they could to make the most of the morning cool. Already these enslaved folks' hands needed Mama's special salve, 'cause their fingers' was raw and bloody from pulling the cotton out of the prickly bolls. We all worked until we couldn't go no farther. More than once, I was so tired I fell asleep face first into my supper plate.

Like I'd conjured him out of the morning mist, Overseer John 'bout run me over, galloping fast. Thanks to Scout's warning yelp, I dodged him but the firewood scattered everywhere. I squatted and began to stack up my dropped load. Where was Overseer going so all-fired fast? The cornfield? The carpenter's shed? The cotton field? I heard a scream and the crack of the whip. I squinted against the rising sun. A horse and rider crashed through the shoulder-high corn chasing a shadowy figure.

I dumped my armload of wood. Scout and I took off past the cotton to the cornfield. Work stopped. Folks stared. Some fell to their knees and prayed. I was breathing hard by the time I got to Sam. He was moaning and rolling on the ground. Scout growled and nipped at Overseer's horse, making him dance. Sam's back was split open and blood ran down into the dirt. He pulled his knees up under him, his arms and hands protecting his head.

"Stop!" I yelled.

The horse pawed the ground and Overseer screamed, "Get out my way, boy. Lemme do my job!" Scout growled and crouched.

I squatted over Sam's body, shielding him from Overseer's crazy. "What's he done?"

"Not your business, Peter." The wicked whip split the air. "Just 'cause you and your folks is the master's favorites, don't mean you won't feel this lash if you step out of line, like Sam here."

"Yes, sir." I stood up and faced Overseer, my head bowed. He was like a wolf. You never looked him in the eye, unless you wanted to get tore apart. "Hear me out, sir. Sam is Dover Hall's only carpenter. If'n he's hurt bad and can't work, Massa Dover ain't gonna like it."

"Don't tell me how to do my job, boy!" Silence. But I could see my words soaking into Overseer John's stubbornness. He lowered the whip. "Sam forgot his place. Caught him fixing up his cabin instead of getting started on his chores this morning. Master Dover don't put up with slaves who forget their place. 'Member that boy, even if you is Peter Farrow, Jr." He kicked his horse into a trot towards the big house. Most likely to tell Massa Dover that Sam and me was causing trouble.

I ripped a strip from my cotton shirt and pressed it gently to Sam's bloody back. He squirmed and moaned, too weak to stand up. A couple of men helped me drag Sam to the quarters. We laid him on his stomach 'cross the cornhusk mattress. Overseer got him with four deep lash marks.

I tore away his shredded shirt. "Sam you gonna be okay? I'll send Mama with her special healing salve. I gotta get. Overseer John will be looking for an excuse to lay the whip on me." Sam's eyes was closed. The bed shook, he was trembling so bad. Scout and I hurried to fetch the wood and get on to the cook house, where we'd be out of sight of

Overseer. I dashed up the back steps, making the quilt that hung on the fence flutter. Mama was inside on her knees scrubbing the brick floor.

"Land sakes, child, is the devil hisself chasing you?" Mama rested back on her heels. She mopped sweat from her forehead with her apron.

I dropped my sticks in the wood box. "Yep, a demon named John." Scout plopped down on Mama's clean floor, tongue hanging out.

Mama stood up, wringing out her scrubbing rag in the bucket. "What you done, son?"

"I had to help Sam, Mama." I slumped into a chair. "Overseer John whupped him just for working on his cabin first thing this morning instead of starting in on his carpenter jobs."

"I'll check in on Sam." Mama hugged me. "My salve will help ease the pain."

"Me and some others got him to his cabin. He got four lashes 'fore I could get to him."

"Son, I's proud of you for risking yourself for Sam. Got the Farrow blood running through your veins for sure. Meanwhile you get yourself upstairs in the sewing parlor. It's time I told you 'bout our family secret now that you is near on twelve years old."

I followed her outside while she dumped her mop water. "What secret you talking 'bout?" I looked up. Mama was back in the kitchen rummaging around on the shelf with her doctoring bottles. "Is the secret 'bout Papa's overnight 'smithing trips?" I had noticed Papa was coming back later and later from his blacksmith jobs. Most times he'd get in 'bout daybreak. When I had asked why he worked all night, Papa had explained Massa was loaning him out to other plantations that didn't have a blacksmith. I frowned, searching my mind for anything else different or strange. "Or is it 'bout those nonsense verses, you and Papa make me say and swear not to talk 'bout?"

"Both. Now I got to see Sam. Get yourself to the sewing parlor." Mama hung up her apron. "Overseer won't think to look for you there this time of the day." She hooked her herb basket over her arm. "Most of the house help is busy, gathering eggs, feeding chickens, and milking. No one should be 'round to ask why you in the house. "

I hung back. "Mama, I don't have no time for secrets right now. I got real trouble here. Overseer John's got it out for me. What am I gonna do?"

Mama headed towards the quarters, but stopped and turned around. Shaking a finger at me, her black eyes had fire in them, burning me up. "This secret is the Farrow family's mission. You is old enough now to do your part."

My shoulders sagged and I turned towards the big house. Don't she understand I is on Overseer's bad side now? This was my problem. Nothin' to do with Papa's extra blacksmithin' jobs or the strange verses. I was worried 'bout Overseer stalking me! But I knew better than to argue with Mama. Vexation rolled off me like ocean waves at high tide.

I ground my teeth and stomped down the worn brick path ignoring the massive flower gardens between the cookhouse and the big house. Massa allowed Dover's Gullah girls to sell flowers and woven sweet grass baskets at the Charlestown Flower Market. The sweet smell of the honeysuckle bushes helped to calm me. By the time I passed the swaying purple wisteria blooms, I was more relaxed. I whispered the nonsense verses I was drilled on since I was old 'nough to talk.

> *"The Monkey Wrench turned the Wagon Wheel toward Canada on Bear's Paw trail to the Crossroads.*
> *Once they got to the Crossroads, they dug a Log Cabin on the ground.*
> *Shoofly told them to dress up in cotton and satin Bow Ties and go to the cathedral church, get married and exchange double wedding rings.*
> *Flying Geese stay on the Drunkard's Path and follow the Stars."*
>
> —from Hidden in Plain View, by Jacqueline Tobin and Dr. Robert Dobard

Monkey Wrench Pattern

Chapter

2

I stepped inside the back door and listened. All was quiet. Wasn't skeeter time yet. Soon Massa Dover and his family would be gone for months. Every summer the family went up North so they wouldn't get the yellow fever from skeeters. But today the white folks must have gone into Charlestown.

I marched into the massive front hall and stood in the center. I planted my feet on the peacock-blue rug in the center of the octagon shaped house. Hands on my hips, I gazed up past all four floors to the dome-shaped skylight with its colored glass. The sun bounced off the three-tiered, crystal chandelier, throwing rainbows on the floor, the walls, and me. I stretched out my arms and spun 'round on my chicken legs. My caramel-colored body shimmered with shades of red, green, yellow and blue. Maybe everybody is all the same color under the sun.

My thoughts slid back to Emily, the Master's daughter. When we was young'uns, we spent many a day spinning and dancing under this dome's rainbows. I 'membered the day we hopscotched over these colorful diamond shapes and bumped into a table, breaking a fancy vase. We claimed Scout did it to get out of trouble.

Now we is both 'bout to be twelve. But unlike me Em be white as a lily with honey-colored curls. We growed up together like brother and sister. I smiled, thinking back on days we made mud pies down by the creek, built stick houses, weaved flower crowns to give to our mamas, and played hide and seek all 'round Dover plantation. We had the run of the place.

When Em took her tutoring lessons, the Missus let me sit by her and learn my letters too. Mama and Papa were surprised. In these parts, slaving folks like us wasn't allowed to read. Missus Dover warned me I was to hide my book learning when visitors was 'round.

I taught Em a few things, too; like how to climb trees with a rope. We could shimmy up a tree 'fore cook noticed we had sneaked food out the kitchen. We had many a tree top snack. Our best times was sitting on the marble steps of the big house's wrap-around veranda guzzling ice cold tea and munching on cook's hot, buttered biscuits. Can't 'member the last time Em and I had an adventure.

Massa or Missus Dover always be calling for Em to come do something when we is walking together. If'n Overseer sees us talking, he yells at me to get back to my chores. Em been telling me to pay him no mind, but I never want to get crosswise with him and his whip. Guess it don't matter now. I done got myself on Overseer's bad side today.

I strolled 'round the braided circle rug under the skylight and stopped to look over the Dover coat-of-arms painted on a faded shield. Em 'splained once that this was a symbol that stood for their family. Seemed to me, if'n they had this on their wall in the main hall, the Dovers must be awful proud of their ancestors. Enslaved folks, like my kinsmen and me, were not allowed to show off a symbol of our African ancestors. Massa told Sam he couldn't make drums, 'cause drumming was the way our Ibo African families talked 'cross the miles. But secretly, Sam promised me he'd teach me how to make small talking drums, since the real talking drums was seven feet tall and ten feet long.

"Peter get on up here, 'fore you get caught!" I jumped. Mama was on the first step of one of the iron spiral staircases. Enslaved folks, like us, was expected to use one of the two back staircases. Papa had built all four in the huge hall, 'fore I was ever born.

"Yes'um, Mama. Just 'membering the good times, playing with Em under the dome." I followed her up to the second floor, running my hand along the tight, spiraling rail as we climbed. My heart swelled with pride at Papa's skill. He was known all 'round these parts for his metalwork. Since I could 'member, Massa let Papa take jobs from other plantations and keep his earnings for hisself. He was saving to buy our freedom.

We hurried to the small sewing parlor. I glanced across the angled balcony from the sewing parlor to Em's school room. I had such happy memories of listening to stories, practicing my letters and looking at pictures in her fancy books. Mama dug through a huge sewing basket on the floor and handed me a needle from her pin cushion and a spool of thread. We used white, cotton thread we had spun right here at Dover.

I stuck out my tongue and jabbed the thread at the needle eye. "While you is telling the secret, I'll thread the needles." This had been my chore since I was five years old.

"No," said Mama. "It's high time you learned to lay out the pieces and sew them together. Everyone in the Farrow family got to know how to do this. It's part of the family secret. 'E kwere m j me oke m.'"

I closed one eye trying to line up the thread and needle. "What language you talking, Mama? What's it mean?"

"It is our Ibo tribal promise. It means I agree to do my part." She got quiet and laid her warm hand on my leg. "Listen, Peter. You is almost twelve, so you is old enough to keep a secret. Your Papa and I are Secret Code Keepers. We sew messages into the quilt patterns." She shot me her no-nonsense, this-is-serious Momma look.

I was only half listening. I licked the thread to make it slide through the needle eye. "Mama, I is too worried 'bout Overseer's crazy temper. Just let me do the knot tying. I can't be thinking 'bout laying out the quilt pieces today."

Mama grabbed both my hands and forced me to look at her. "We is expecting you, Peter, to carry on our work someday."

I dropped the needle. "Secrets in the quilts? What did you say? Something 'bout Secret Keepers?" Now she had my attention. "Mama, what you talking 'bout?"

Mama smiled and patted my arm. "Like I said, your Papa and I are Secret Code Keepers. We sew secret messages into the quilt patterns. Let's start with the knot tying. Sometimes the knots tied on top of a quilt mean months. Three knots close together is March, the third month of a new year. Other times the knots is spaced apart to stand for miles 'tween places."

"Months until what? Miles to where?"

"Peter, this is all part of being a Secret Code Keeper." She got up, closed the double doors and handed me some cut pieces. "Help me lay out this quilt top on the floor. Think of it like a puzzle."

I got down on my knees spreading out the cut cloth. "What is a Secret Code Keeper?"

"I's getting to it. Back in Iboland, I worked in the textile house 'fore I was your age. I learned to make dyes from plants, like Indigo, to color the threads blue or purple." Mama sat cross-legged beside me and laid out four strips and four triangles. "This here is one of our Ibo designs. It's called the Monkey Wrench. You make a box with the strips and then sew the triangles onto each of the four corners."

"The words, Monkey Wrench are in the poem you and Papa make me recite every day." I laid out the pattern, and began to pin it.

Mama grabbed my chin and forced me to look at her eyes. "Pay attention. Each pattern we sew tells a secret message to our people to help them escape to freedom. Peter, you can't talk 'bout this to anyone, except Papa and me. You understand?"

My mouth dropped open. "Messages in the quilts?" This got something to do with Papa's late nights? Em would love this, I thought. 'Cause Mama's quilts was on the beds in Dover Hall, right under the Massa and Mistress' noses. "Em loves secrets. She'd not tell. I is sure of it."

Mama set down her sewing and grabbed me by the shoulders. "No! Never tell Emily. Our lives depend on it." I didn't understand it all, but I knew better than to cross Mama. She let go, but kept her eyes locked on me. "Not all enslaved folks have generous owners, like our Massa. Most are starved, work from 'cain't see to cain't see' and some are tortured if'n they don't make their quotas. All of us want to be free. But some will die if'n they don't get to freedom land soon."

I made tight, neat stitches to hold the quilt block together. I knew if I got sloppy, Mama would rip it out and make me do it again. I sighed. This secret would be another wall coming up 'tween Em and me.

Mama laid out more quilt blocks while she talked. "Your Papa and I help folks get to a safe place on the Underground Railroad. In our Ibo homeland, the Monkey Wrench was a caravan leader who led folks through jungles and deserts by watching the stars. To us, it means a person who knows the land and can lead a group to a safe house. Here, the monkey wrench is a tool used by a blacksmith. But on the Underground Railroad, we is talking 'bout a guide called a conductor. Papa is a respected Monkey Wrench in these parts. While he's repairing tools, shoeing horses, building iron gates and fancy staircases on nearby plantations, he is figuring out the best ways to go north. When we hang this Monkey Wrench quilt on the fence, we is telling enslaved folks the conductor will soon be leading a group to freedom."

I stopped stitching and looked up. "You mean besides Papa being a preacher and a blacksmith, he's helping folks escape?" Mama nodded. My thoughts ran around like a wild horse. "What happens if'n the Missus comes by while we sewing this here monkey wrench pattern?"

Mama winked at me. "We tell her it's the Churndash pattern. 'Cause it looks like the barrel paddles used to churn cream into butter."

I glanced sideways at Mama. "What else you and Papa been hiding from me?"

Mama dug in the scrap basket and pulled out a quilt block with strips arranged around a small circle in the middle. "There are ten quilt codes in all. The same ones you say in the verse. This here is the Wagon Wheel Pattern."

"What's the secret message in that one?" I asked.

Mama shuffled some cut pieces. "It means Papa will be hiding young'uns and elders in his wagon with the false bottom."

"False bottom?" I dropped my quilt block and stared at Mama. "Papa's work wagon has a hidey- hole?"

"Only way you'd know is if'n you saw the breathing holes drilled underneath." Mama laid out cloth pieces showing me how to make the Wagon Wheel block. "There's a hidden space in the back of the wagon bed."

"He built it hisself? Ouch!" I had stabbed myself with the needle. "What other secrets you got, Mama?" I wiped the drop of blood on my britches.

Mama hugged me. "We just getting started, son. I think you is old 'nough to become a Secret Code Keeper 'long with us."

"Can I ride in the hidey hol...?" I didn't finish 'cause Sarie opened the door. Mama raised her eyebrows, gave me 'the look' and shook her head. I knowed she was telling me "don't trust Sarie," even if she is a slave lady and one of us.

"I just come for Peter," said Sarie. "Overseer John tole me to fetch you to work in the dairy. We need someone to help with the churning, since Millie's down sick."

I handed Mama my Monkey Wrench quilt block and winked. "Mama, got to go work in the dairy." I leaned in and whispered, "Gotta go do some 'churnin' so I is gonna 'dash' outta of here."

Mama elbowed me and chuckled. "Run along. Overseer be the boss." Sarie frowned at our strange conversation and motioned for me to follow her downstairs.

Wagon Wheel Pattern

Chapter 3

Before today, I had never worked in the dairy. The dairy was a rough stone building, set back in the grove of magnolia trees. I loved the feel of the cool, brick floor on my bare feet. The breeze blew through the tall windows. Most days, the dairy was the only cool place to escape the suffocating heat of the summer. After fetching wood for cook's stove, I milked Bessie and Mort, our milk cows. Then I toted buckets of foaming milk to the dairy. During the day, whenever cook needed butter, cream, eggs, or milk from the dairy, I fetched it to the cookhouse.

Sarie pointed to a corner with a skinny wooden barrel and a three-legged stool. "The butter churn's there." I sat down and looked at a long wooden stick that poked from the hole in the top. Sarie stepped over and tilted the barrel. She sloshed it around, listening. "Cream's been poured in ready for churnin'. Peter, you grip the handle here and pump up and down. When the pushing and the pulling gets hard, means the butter is ready."

I wrapped my calloused hands 'round the pole. "Like this?"

Sarie pushed my knees together, tight against the barrel. "Easier if you hold it steady with your legs. Now get to it. We got plenty of cream waiting in the cellar for you to churn."

I sighed and pinned the barrel between my knees. I pumped the paddle up and down until my arms burned. When I couldn't pump no more, Sarie stopped me and lifted the lid. Golden, sticky globs of butter floated like islands in a milky sea. She scraped the butter out of the churn, then sent me down the stone steps to the cellar. A natural spring bubbled up from below ground.

"Fetch another gallon of milk," Sarie yelled. "Get the jars with the cream floating on top. I'll show you how to strain off the cream."

At the bottom of the steps, I stuck my bare feet into the cold water. It felt like a million tiny needles, but it cooled me down in a hurry. I wished I could hang out here for a while. I studied the gallon jugs of milk lined up on a rock shelf just above the water line. A thick, creamy layer coated the top of the milk.

"Are you lollygagging down there, Peter?" Sarie yelled. "Get a move on and bring me two jars!" I grabbed two with the cream floating like thick soap suds and trudged back up the stone stairs. "Listen up. This here's how you strain out the cream to put it in the churn. Hold this." She handed me a mesh-wire dipper. I held it over the top of a pitcher while she poured the milk through it. The clotted cream stuck in the wire. Sarie knocked the creamy globs loose into the butter churn.

All morning, I toted jugs of milk, strained off cream, and pumped the churn. Leastways I got more chances to stick my feet into the freezing water. Finally, we had four small jars of butter stored down in the cellar. My arms ached from the butter making.

I hurried to the cook house 'cause I had more chores 'fore the noon day meal. Most days, I hauled water from the creek for cooking and washing dishes. Then there was the carrying and chopping wood to feed the hungry woodburning stove.

After the Dover family's meal was done and the dishes was cleared, we slaving folks got to sit down and eat our noon day meal. I was 'bout to take my first bite, when Will, our shoofly, came in bringing the last of the dirty dishes from the dining room. He took off his white gloves and pulled up a chair real close. "I heard the family talking at the table 'bout a new Fugitive Slave Act." Mama got up and bolted the cook house doors. When ShooFly had news, folks listened.

Since I was little, I wanted to be Will. He got to wear pressed, clean clothes. He got to serve the white folks in the dining room. Until the family was at the table, he kept the food platters warm in the squat, iron stove facing the fireplace.

After Will set out the fancy platters and bowls, Massa Dover said the prayer. Then Will would step back in the corner and work the rope pulley that was fastened to a paddle. The paddle swung above the dinner table, shooing the flies off the food. That's why white folks call him ShooFly. To us he was Will.

In the hot months, the floor-to-ceiling windows were open to catch any breeze. Bugs came and went like bees to a hive. Folks said Will was the best shoofly. He stood still as a statue for hours. Only his gloved hands moved, pulling the rope. The family and their visitors paid him no mind and plumb forgot he was there. So he listened in on their table talk and passed the important parts on to us slavin' folks.

Sarie shifted in her creaky chair. "What you mean, Will? We already got a Fugitive Slave Act."

Will leaned forward and whispered. "I ain't talking 'bout the old 1793 law that got us free once we crossed the Mason Dixon Line. That's 'bout to change. This new Fugitive Slave Act says runaways can be captured and brought back to their masters, even if'n they crossed the Mason Dixon Line into the free north states! Patrollers will get paid to track us and drag us back to be punished. Or killed." Will stopped talking and stared at his plate. The room got quiet. Some folks wiped tears. Most stopped eating. Others closed their eyes and whispered prayers.

I reached for my wood piece. My mind wondered back to when Papa gave it to me for my tenth birthday."This here came from the first Ibo canoe I made in Iboland when I was 'bout your age. Keep it with you always, son. It is your Ogbe."

I took it. "Just looks like a piece of polished wood to me." It nestled in my palm as if it was home. I held it up close and touched it's pointed ends. "What'd you call it?"

"Ogbe. It stands for protection and the giver of life." Papa took it and cradled it in his fingers while he rubbed his thumb over the middle. "Sam polished it smooth and carved the ends to look like a canoe."

For the last two years, I had kept it deep in my pocket so Overseer would never find it. When you is an enslaved boy in South Carolina, you needs all the help you can get.

"What you mean Will?" Mama asked. "Folks can't get free if'n they get 'cross the River Jordan no more?"

Will never looked up. "We got to go all the way north to

Canada." He scooted his plate away and buried is head in his crossed arms. It felt like a dark cloud settled 'round us.

"Where's the River Jordan?" I asked. "Can't we go a different way to get free?"

Bonna, the cook, explained. "The River Jordan, like the promised land in the Bible, is what we call the River between Kentucky and Ohio. Once you crossed over into Ohio you was free. But no more."

Mama patted my arm. "Peter, this new law says we got to go many more miles to be safe. Getting to the River Jordan and crossing into Ohio was hard, but Canada is hundreds more miles north. More chance of getting caught, starving to death, or being lost." Mama stood up and straightened her apron. "Come on, Peter, let's take a plate out to your Papa."

I'd just taken a few bites, but I wasn't hungry no more. I didn't know where these places was 'cause I never been off the plantation. But I knowed Papa's conductor job on the Underground was 'bout to get more dangerous. I followed Mama over to the cook stove.

The minute we was out of earshot, she whispered, "Peter, while I is dipping up food for Papa, you run to our cabin and fetch the ShooFly quilt. We got to let folks know if they is thinking 'bout running, they got to get ready quick."

I took off like a shot and rushed back. After I handed her the quilt, I put my hands on my knees breathing hard. Between breaths, I asked, "Mama, how do our enslaved folks know what the quilt codes mean?"

Mama took down the Wagon Wheel quilt, folded it, and laid it aside. "Do you pay any mind to your Papa's preaching on Sundays?"

I dug my toe in the dirt, not wanting to confess. "Well, uh, in the Praise House I sleep mostly, but in the arbor, I sit on the back bench picking and eating grapes. I don't pay no mind."

Momma frowned. "Peter, you gonna be sitting up by me on the front row, from now on 'till Jesus come. Don't forget you not too big for a whupping with a willow tree branch."

"Yes, Momma." I kept my head down. "I be all ears and eyes during Papa's service from now on."

Momma nodded. "If you'd been listening, Peter, you'd seen the spirit move folks to start shouting, talking in what sounds like gibberish. White folks call it speaking in tongues. Other times our kinsmen are passing messages 'bout the codes."

Mama handed me one end of the ShooFly Quilt. "Listen close, next time." She stepped away from me to stretch it to its full length. "You may hear something 'bout the quilt codes. Other times we whisper while we doing our chores 'round the farm."

While I helped her spread the quilt 'cross the wooden fence, she explained the message in the ShooFly pattern. "This pattern says ShooFly is telling things that will help them stay ahead of the patrollers. Like when the family be going on a trip or will be busy with their big dinners and balls." Mama smoothed out the quilt. "When the white folks is busy, conductors got time to give the runaways a head start 'fore anyone notices."

I rubbed my hand over the quilt, picturing Papa leading our kinsmen to freedom by moonlight, always looking over his shoulder for patrollers. "Mama, I wanna go with Papa on his next trip."

Mama pulled me into a hug "Oh no, Peter. Too dangerous. Pattyrollers got man-eating dogs! Folks that is caught helping runaways, no matter their skin color, gets hanged. Or worse." Mama handed me Papa's plate covered in a dish cloth.

I gave her a one arm hug, careful not to spill the food. "Mama, I'll be twelve in a few days. Em told me Massa is gonna send me to work with Sam to learn to be a carpenter. If'n I can do that, I is big enough to help Papa on the Underground."

ShooFly Pattern

Chapter 4

Long before I got to the blacksmith shed, I heard Papa's hammer pounding a rhythm into the red-hot metal on the anvil. When he saw me, Papa stopped pumping the bellows and the flames died down to a smolder. Sweat ran down his muscled arms. He dropped the finished horseshoe into a bucket of cool water. It sizzled as he wiped the sweat from his face with a rag. After washing up in the water barrel, he took the tin plate and sat on a nearby tree stump. "Smells good, son. I's hungry."

I sat 'cross from him on the ground, picking grass and tossing it in the air. "Papa, I can help you on the Underground." Papa stopped chewing, so I talked fast 'fore he shut me up. "Mama been telling 'bout you both being keepers of a secret code. I's ready. I is 'bout twelve." Papa put down his plate and shook his head. But I kept talking. "At lunch, Shoofly done told us 'bout a new Fugitive Slave Act. You is gonna need more help."

Papa took a long drink from the water dipper. "Tell me more 'bout this new Fugitive Slave Act." While Papa cleaned his plate, I told him 'bout runaways being forced to go all the way to Canada to be free. Papa was real quiet, a sure sign he was thinking up a plan. I jumped when he asked, "You say you been learning the quilt codes with Mama?"

"Yep, I knows three patterns, Monkey Wrench, Wagon Wheel and ShooFly."

"You not ready, son. It ain't 'bout how grown you is or how strong you is, it's 'bout what you know to keep folks safe. You got to learn 'bout the other seven quilt codes first."

My chin dropped to my chest. "I have to know all ten? Gonna take forever!"

Papa set down his tin plate and looked me straight in the eyes. "If'n you is going to be a secret code keeper, you got to know everything. Did you know Massa Dover got insurance on Will, Sam and me, so if'n any of us got hurt or died, he'd get money to replace us with another slave? If'n I is dead or caught, we gotta make sure you is the one to step in, so you and Mama can carry on our work. Massa Dover would likely let you take my place, 'cause he could keep the insurance money and not have to buy another slave."

Caught? Dead?, I thought as I stared at him. I looked at my Papa with different eyes. His honey colored arms were muscled up. He was the tallest of us enslaved folks on the plantation, with legs thick as tree trunks. His smarts showed when he built fancy ironwork, like Dover Hall's twisting staircases. I couldn't imagine any pattyroller catching him.

I wandered over to Papa's anvil and tried to lift the iron hammer. I couldn't move it an inch. That proved I wasn't strong 'nough. But was I brave 'nough or smart 'nough to fill Papa's shoes? I could never replace Papa and I didn't want to.

Papa swallowed his last bite. "Come on 'round back and I'll let you feed Hampton and Mamie this apple." Papa led me to the lean-to attached to the blacksmith shed. His prized pair of sleek, black horses stood in their stalls. "These two are the strongest and fastest 'round these parts." Hampton let me stroke his soft nose, but Mamie turned her head away even when I offered the apple. "It takes her a bit longer to warm up to folks," he said. "These two saved my hide many a time. Not only 'cause they is fast, but they is smart, too. They knowed all the shortcuts back to Dover Hall."

Papa took me to the stall where he kept his wagon. I circled 'round it but couldn't see any trap door. Then Papa removed a wide board 'cross the tailgate. There below the wagon bed was a false bottom. The hidey-hole was long and narrow. "I pile my blacksmith bellows, tool crates and feed sacks on top."

I imagined riding cramped, face down, and breathing dust kicked up by the wagon wheels. "Don't look none too comfortable."

"Comfort and running don't go together, son." I helped Papa slide the wide board back in place across the hidey-hole. He strolled to the front of the blacksmith shed, thinking out loud. "Guess we can't take folks to the Crossroads no more."

"Crossroads?" I asked.

"It's where three Indian trails crisscross in one place. Runaways gotta choose which way to go; west to Iowa, north to Ohio or Michigan. If 'n they go south to Florida they can live with the Seminole Indians."

I sat on the stump and watched Papa pump up the bellows again, making the fire hot enough to melt metal. "What you gonna do, 'bout this new Fugitive Slave Law?"

He stopped working and adjusted his knee length leather apron. "We all come to a crossroads in our life, son. It be tempting to close your eyes to how the plantation masters treat our kinsmen. It'd be easier to hunker down and stay out of harm's way. But if'n I was running, I'd want someone, a Monkey Wrench, to lead me down the hard road towards freedom. Things is 'bout to get tougher, son. But we'll see our way through. Guess I'll have to convince Massa that I be needin' to take on extra jobs farther away from Dover Hall. It'd give me time to get folks to safe houses on up the line."

"Mama was talking 'bout a safe house. What is it?" I asked.

"It's part of the seven quilt codes you don't know yet. Now run 'long and ask your Mama." Papa turned back to making nails from the heated scrap metal.

I trudged back to the big house. Ugh! More time in the sewing parlor. Just past the dairy, I spied Em carrying her fishing pole. "Come on, Peter. Let's go fishing," she begged. "It's so hot today. We can dangle our feet in the cold water."

I glanced 'round. "Em, Overseer is watching me like a spider waitin' to catch a fly."

Em rolled her eyes. "If you're with me, he'll leave you be. Quit worrying."

"Okay. Just for a short spell." I dashed off to fetch my pole and spear.

Em called out, "Hurry, Peter. I'll meet you at our favorite spot." She walked away, swinging her bucket of worms, her honey-colored curls bouncing like wagon springs. "If we're lucky, we can take Cook some catfish for supper tonight."

It was only afternoon, but I was dog tired. My head felt it would burst from the code keeper secrets, looking over my shoulder for Overseer John, and worrying 'bout the fugitive law. I looked 'round to see if anyone was watching, then pushed my way through the curtain of moss dangling from the huge trees. The moss hung over the creek bank and hid our favorite flat rock. Hopefully, Overseer wouldn't find me here. I rolled up my ragged pants, slid down the rock, and waded into the cool water. I stood perfectly still and held my spear steady.

Em cast her line from the rock and stuck her toes in the cool water. It almost felt comfortable 'tween us, the way it used to be. "Peter, have you heard about the Spring Ball? It's coming right up."

I frowned. "Comes 'round every year. How could I forget? Have to work my tail off getting ready for it."

She batted her eyes at me. "I like to call it a soiree. I'll be the belle of the ball in my new emerald green dress."

I smiled. "I'd say you is a whippersnapper."

"Peter!" she yelled and splashed me with water.

"Shush, you is scaring the fish." I put my finger to my lips and whispered. "Em, your fancy parties just mean extra work for us in the big house."

Em raised her eyebrows. "The Spring Ball is after your birthday. So you'll be working with Sam by then, learning to be a carpenter."

"Cain't wait!" I jumped up and did a high-stepping jig, splashing Em with cold water.

"Now look who's scaring the fish." Em giggled. "What are you doing?"

I winked at her. "This here is my happy dance."

"More like a hurt toad trying to hop." Em propped her pole up against the rock. "I been practicing my ball dancing. Let me show you how it's done." She hoisted me out of the water onto the flat rock. She took both my hands and looked down. "Now start on this foot..."

Massa Dover stepped through our willow tree curtain and snarled, "Emily, what are you doing?" I dropped her hands and stepped back. Massa Dover crossed is arms. "You two up to no good?"

"No Sir." I grabbed my spear. "Just fishing and talking and, uh..." My voice trailed off to a whisper, " ...a little dancing."

"I was showing him some steps," Em interrupted. "Peter doesn't know the first thing about party dancing. Someone had to teach him." She shook her head like I was a lost cause.

"Peter don't have any need of dancing," Massa growled. He turned to me. "You got work waiting on you, right?"

I nodded. "Yes, sir."

Massa Dover frowned. "Emily, Mother is looking all over for you. You best be getting to the house, now." He disappeared back through the willow tree curtain.

I swallowed a bitter taste in my mouth and waded back in the water. I threw my spear in the mud as hard as I could! Why was he mad at Em and me? We was just having a good time, like we used to do when we was little. I jerked my spear free. Em shrugged and disappeared through the moss curtain, following her daddy.

I trudged back to the slave quarters. I sensed change coming like when a hurricane was headed our way. But I was helpless to stop it.

Crossroads Pattern

Chapter 5

I woke up the next morning to the smell of bacon, biscuits, fried apples, and grits. Papa was drinking coffee from his tin cup while Mama filled my plate. She set it on our sturdy wooden table that Sam had built.

"Mornin' Peter," Papa said between bites.

I popped up. "What day is it? My birthday is just 'round the corner."

Mama stirred the grits in the pot hanging from the fireplace spit. "Six more days, Peter. Go on now and wash up 'fore you come to the table."

I made a trip to the outhouse, and then filled my pitcher at the water barrel. Back inside the cabin, I scooped water onto my face and hands from the chipped washbasin, a cast off from the big house. I pulled up a chair and dived into Mama's big breakfast. The woman could sure cook! She was practiced up 'cause she helped with the cooking in the big house when she wasn't cleaning and sewing.

"Sam is teaching me to whittle clothes pins."

Papa squeezed my shoulder. "Clothes pins is good practice." He cleaned his plate. "Mama, I'll fetch you a bucket of water for washing up. Peter, better be quick 'bout milking Bessie and Mort, 'cause you got lots of water hauling today."

"It's wash day?" My shoulders sagged. Wash day was the worst. Only good thing 'bout it was it happened only once a week. I sat up straight and grinned. This here would be the last time I'd be helping with wash day! 'Cause I'd be a carpenter 'prentice next week. Twelve couldn't get here fast 'nough! I finished breakfast and dropped my dishes into Mama's wash bucket. The sun was peeking over the horizon as I hurried to the barn. The milking had to get done first.

After I let Bessie and Mort out to pasture, I strapped the wooden yoke over my shoulders. Empty water buckets dangled from each end. By the time the sun was full up, I had filled the wash pot half full and the yoke had rubbed the back of my neck raw. I sure hoped Mama had some of her healing salve saved up. After what felt like a thousand trips to the creek, both the wash pot and the rinse pot were full. After fetching water, I helped carry loads of dirty clothes, linens, blankets and quilts to the wash house.

My next job was to keep plenty of wood piled up for the fire boiling under the wash pot. I got no idea how Papa made those huge iron pots. They was big 'nough folks could swim in them. Maybe Hampton and Mamie pulled them 'cross the ground from the blacksmith shed to the wash house. After I stacked up plenty of firewood, the young girls built up the fire under the wash pot and fed it wood so it boiled the clothes all day long. If'n they had to wait on me, for water or wood, those girls hollerd at me like a stuck pig. Once the water got boiling, the girls dropped in the clothes and stirred in the lye soap chips. The strongest women took turns stirring with canoe-size paddles. After a bit, they carried clothes from the wash pot to the rinse pot. Then they wrung them out by twisting. Lastly they'd shake out everything and hang it all on the fences and bushes to dry. We was all weary by the time wash day was done. Mostly 'cause my chores doubled. Some days, I tried to get on a little faster, but if'n I hustled too much I just sloshed water all the way to the pots. I learned to just work steady, no matter how much had to get done.

Soon as my part of wash day chores was done, I hustled to the big house to work the noon day meal. I fetched wood for the cook stove and carried the food dishes to Will in the dining room. Then it was clean up time and refilling the fireplace wood boxes in all the rooms of the big house. As the sun kissed the horizon, I brushed and fed the Massa's horses, shoveled the stalls, and helped weed the vegetable garden. I never had time to get to the sewing parlor on wash days.

Basket Pattern

Chapter 6

By suppertime, I was back at the big house to help with the family's evening meal. I trudged up the back porch steps and noticed the Crossroads quilt flapping in the breeze. As I wondered why Mama had taken down the ShooFly quilt, she rushed through the door and 'bout ran me over. "Mama, why did you change the qu..."

"Peter, go back to your Papa, now. Tell him to meet me in the Praise House. No the grape arbor! We gots to get some runaways out, quick." She shoved a basket in my hands. "When you get to the arbor act like you picking grapes for cook."

What was happening? Mama looked panicked. I stretched out my skinny chicken legs and flew past Dover folks going 'bout their evening work. Sarie grabbed for me as I sprinted by her. "Peter! Come carry this cheese up to the big house. Cook needs it for supper."

"Cain't now," I yelled over my shoulder. "Got some runawa..." Oh shut my mouth! Mama warned me not to trust Sarie. "I mean I got to run. Business for Massa." I heard her yelling my name but I never slowed. I was on code keepers business.

A few minutes later, Mama, Papa and I met in the grape arbor. This was Papa's church house in the summertime. I looked up at the curling grape vines twisting through the overhead arches and imagined folks whispering 'bout the quilt codes, explaining the messages.

Papa frowned. "Eliza, what's wrong?"

"Abraham ran with a group from the Johnson plantation last night. Patrollers caught him. Those with him got away."

Papa bowed his head. "God save us all."

Mama's lips quivered. "They hung him. Abraham's widow buried him in secret. Even though she's grieving, she wants his death to mean something. She's counting on you to save the others that are scattered and hiding."

Silence.

I fidgeted and reached deep into my pocket for my Ogbe. I slid my thumb over the smoth wood. "What you gonna do, Papa?"

Mama dried her tears on her apron. Papa's eyes narrowed as he gazed at the sunset. I knew he was thinking hard 'bout how to save those people from the patrollers. Papa shoved back his straw hat and turned 'round to us. "I got permission to work at the Johnson's plantation. I didn't know we would need an escape plan, but God did. He opened up a way. We can sneak those folks out in a funeral procession."

Mama dropped a cluster of grapes into her basket. "Sure we can pull it off? We gots to move fast. We want to make it look like we is going to bury Abraham. Patrollers know dead bodies don't keep. Tell folks to gather tomorrow night?"

Papa twirled his sweat-stained hat in his hands "Yeah, in the apple orchard behind the Johnson's barn. I'll get the word out at the Johnson place to folks who can pass it on to Abraham's runaways. Anyone going with us needs to wear their mourning clothes. We can hide someone in Abraham's empty coffin and hide a young'un or two in the wagon."

Mama dropped some grapes in my basket. "I'll bring a mourning cloth to cover the coffin and wagon. At first light, the runaways will follow in the funeral march. We won't have much time. Can we get as far as the crossroads?"

Papa shrugged. "We ain't never done this. With that new Fugitive Slave Act breathing down our neck, we got to rethink things. We can't get folks as far as the North Star Station 'cross the River Jordan, but we can get them to the closest safe house."

"What's the North Star Station?" I asked.

Mama sat down on a bench, fanning her face with her apron. "A man named John Parker is a conductor that has saved thousands of folks. He is a respectable owner of a foundry in town. His house is on the north bank of the Ohio River. When he sees runaways struggling to get 'cross, he rescues them with his boat. Or if they's running for the shore, he meets them and ferries them 'cross."

Papa sat down next to Mama and fanned himself with his hat. "Hidden in a row of bushes, John built a steel staircase that leads straight down to a secret cellar."

Mama handed me a cluster of grapes in case someone was watching us. "When John sees the lantern signal, he rushes the runaways up the hill to a conductor's house. It's called the North Star Station."

Papa settled his hat on his head. "Since we is leaving before the Sunday meeting, we got to get the word out another way. Liza, hang out the Basket quilt and Tumbling Block quilt to let folks know."

"I wanna help, Papa!" I sat down on the bench beside him. "I'm ready."

Papa patted me on the head. "Peter, you spread the word. But only to those thinking 'bout running. Mama will let you know who you can trust."

I jumped up and did my toad-hopping jig. I got a job on the Underground! Then I got serious and shook Papa's calloused hand. "Papa, you can count on me."

"Be careful, son." He hugged me. "This is dangerous business."

Mama finished filling her grape basket. "We got to be careful who gets wind of this. Some enslaved folks would sell us out to the Massa and Overseer."

For the next two days, I plumb forgot 'bout my birthday. While I carried and fetched, I whispered 'bout the funeral escape, but only to the folks Mama trusted. The funeral procession lasted for three days and nights. A young mother and her baby was hid in Abraham's coffin and two young'uns rode in the wagon's hidey-hole. Mama gave them a sleeping potion to keep them quiet. Then she covered the wagon bed with a black cloth.

Papa knew the towns 'long the way. He told every patroller we met we was going to bury Abraham in the next town. That way we kept inching north, one town at a time. As we walked through each town, we cried, hollered, clapped, danced and sang hymns behind the wagon. I didn't know if folks was caterwauling from joy at being closer to freedom land, or 'cause of sadness being parted from their families forever. I figured freedom must have both heartache and happiness tangled up together. Some watchers walked a ways with us. If'n they spotted any family in our group that had been sold away, they'd cling to each other and cry.

After we got the runaways to a safe house, Papa took Mama and I back to Dover Hall a different way than we come. We didn't want patrollers wondering why our group had disappeared. We heard later that all our folks made it to Canada, just days before the 1850 Fugitive Slave Act became law. I smiled when I pictured Abraham dancing on streets of gold, happy his death had freed so many of his kinsmen.

Tumbling Blocks Pattern

Chapter 7

Lately, Papa was traveling more 'tween plantations with Hampton and Mamie. He'd stay away a week or more to work on massive iron gates, or metal staircase banisters, or chandeliers in the big houses on neighboring plantations. Often times, folks from other plantations brought work to Dover for Papa or Sam. He'd spend days just making nails. It takes a lot of nails to keep all the plantation buildings standing. Most owners took all the money their enslaved folks made, but Massa Dover let Papa keep his earned money.

While Papa was gone, Massa let Mama help out over at the Butler Plantation Hospital. It was for enslaved people. Afraid I'd get crossways with Overseer, she asked Massa Dover if'n I could go with her to learn 'bout her healing work. She and Papa were treated good 'cause they had special skills that Massa needed to keep Dover Hall running. He gave his permission, but told Mama we had to be back 'fore dark to avoid any pattyrollers in the area who might steal us.

Next morning, when we took off at sun-up for the Butler Hospital, Mama said, "Peter, now that you be helping as a code keeper, I need to tell you 'bout a few more quilt codes."

I kept pace with her. "Sure Mama."

We stopped at a shady spot in a thick grove of trees and she pulled out a quilt block from the bottom of her basket. "This here is a Log Cabin pattern. It has a small square in the middle and strips of cloth sewed around it like logs. As you add strips, the square gets bigger like you is building a cabin."

"Don't look too hard." I squatted beside her, chewing a piece of sweet grass.

"But it carries an important message." Mama ran her hand across the quilt block to smooth it out. "A dark, colored square in the middle of the Log Cabin block means danger."

I shrugged my shoulders. "Don't we use whatever scraps is left over from clothes making?"

Mama's eyes seemed to catch fire. "The Log Cabin quilt is hung on the fence or bushes next to a safe house. If'n it has a light colored or red center, it means the runaways can come to the door for rest, food and help. But if'n there are slave catchers nearby or hiding in the house, the folks helping the slaves will hang out the Log Cabin quilt with a dark center. The station masters are telling the runaways to keep going, it ain't safe. If'n there's no quilt outside, folks look for a lantern in the window. That's the signal it's safe. No light in the window means don't stop." Mama took a deep breath and gazed out at the trees. "Folks lives depend on these signals and our quilt codes."

I belly flopped onto the grass. "I hope I can 'member all the codes. I don't want to make a mistake and cause folks to get caught."

Mama roughed up my hair. "You got time to learn Peter. But you gots to be careful who you tell 'bout the codes. Never forget there is some of our own kinsmen who will sell us out to patrollers if'n offered 'nough money."

I shivered, picturing my kinsmen walking into a trap. They'd be chained and drug behind a horse back to their owners. Then they'd be tortured or killed.

Mama packed her basket again, putting her healing plants and remedies on top. "Best be on our way." She pointed at something. "Peter, see these spider webs? Grab me some 'long the way. They is great for healing wounds."

I broke off a small branch. It was slow work 'cause when I'd see a good spider web, I had to stop and roll it onto my stick. Mama looked back and nodded. "Peter, we got to hurry on now. There is woman having trouble delivering her babe. I gots some herbs here to ease the pain."

When we got to the hospital we had so much to do we didn't have time to talk 'bout being a secret code keeper. Just 'fore sunset, we left the hospital. The trail we took back to Dover Hall had so many switchbacks it made me dizzy. I was plumb wore out from carrying

Log Cabin Pattern

buckets, fetching water, and dumping slop jars all day. I felt kinda sick from the smell of vomit, blood and death. "Mama, why we taking this zigzag way?"

"Want to show you another quilt pattern," she said over her shoulder. The path was so narrow, we could only walk single file. When we came to a shallow creek, I collapsed on the sandbar and scooped cool creek water onto the back of my neck.

Mama put her woven sweet grass basket into the water. "Son, let's sit a spell." She picked out a shady spot and scooped up a handful of dirt. "Do you see this?"

"Dirt is dirt. I see it every day." I smeared water on my face and frowned at her.

"This sandy, crumbly stuff is Carolina dirt. But as you go north, the dirt changes." Mama fanned herself with her apron. "Nature gives us clues in the stars to where we be. In the way birds fly, and in the dirt. Since we live close to the ocean, the dirt is sandy and scattered with shell pieces. But north of here, in Georgia, the dirt becomes sticky and red. It's clay."

I scooped up a handful of sandy dirt and let it sift through my fingers. I had run barefoot through it my whole life, but I'd never taken the time to feel the tiny shell bits.

Mama continued. "North of Georgia, the dirt becomes blacker and softer. It be rich dirt, river bottom dirt, good for growing different crops."

"Why you telling me this, Mama?" I doodled a picture in the sand with my finger.

"Our people have to run north. But most never been off the plantation. We got no maps. Most cain't read the few signs there is. Runaways have to use the clues in nature to make sure they is always going north. And if you is gonna carry on our work, Peter, you got to teach folks not just the quilt codes but also nature's codes."

I dusted off my hands. "It takes lots of smarts to get to freedomland, don't it?" I swooshed out my breath. "What if I don't 'member to tell folks everything?"

Mama hugged me tight. "Peter you are braver and smarter than you think. Just keep asking questions, and never stop learning."

I smiled. "Here's my first question. Why we taking the long way back to Dover Hall? The path we took this morning was straight as a string, but this one feels like we is going in circles."

Mama dug another quilt block out of her basket. "That is exactly what we doing. Like this crazy pattern in this block. Conductors lead runaways through the woods on a zig-zag path through the underbrush. Never on trails. They crisscross shallow creeks whenever they can."

I took a closer look at the quilt block. "Why?"

"Crossing water throws the dogs off the scent." Mama got a faraway look in her eyes. "In my Ibo homeland, we was taught evil always goes in a straight line. To be safe, we backtracked and circled when traveling through the jungle. My mama and I painted the walls of our hut in a zig-zag pattern to protect our family from evil spirits. As a chil', I saw adults paint or cut this crooked design on their bodies." A tear slid down her soft brown cheek.

I wiped away her tear with my thumb. "You miss your homeland?"

Mama sighed and then got busy spreading a red-checked handkerchief over a log. "Let's rest a bit and eat." After praying for Jesus' protection of all captive people, we ate fried chicken legs, a couple of sweet taters, and chunks of cornbread. Then Mama threw our chicken bones into her sweet grass basket floating in the creek.

"What you doin', Mama?" I said around a mouthful of food.

"Trapping us some fish for a fish fry."

I frowned. "If'n we need fish I would a toted my fishing pole. I cain't spear a fish as good as Papa."

Mama laughed. "No need. I slide the top of my fishing basket open and the fish swim in to nibble at the chicken bones. Then I slide it shut and pull the basket from the water. The water drains out and we got us a fish supper."

I grinned. "Ain't you the smart one, Mama." We watched the fireflies flashing their lights in the early evening. "Tell me 'bout how you and Papa got here to Dover?"

Mama chewed her last bite, rinsed her hands in the creek and wiped them on her apron. "I was a child. One day, a band of both black and white men came upriver. My Nigerian village was on a trade route, so we was used to welcoming strangers. Our tribe invited them to stop. We shared our kola nut soup from the oha, nsala and akwu plants we growed. I 'member dancing with bird feathers braided into my hair. I can still hear my bell bracelets jingling on my ankles and arms." Mama looked at me with a sad smile.

"Did the strangers trade?" I asked trying to picture life in Iboland. Would I have danced, if I was born there? Would I have helped the metalsmith make the bells for the tribal regalia?

"Oh, yes. The strangers had many pretty things to trade. Our tribe spoke many languages, but we had never heard English words. We talked with motions and signs." Mama hesitated and covered her face with her hands.

I laid my head on her shoulder. "Go on, Mama."

She sucked in a deep breath and relaxed her fisted hands. "Then the traders passed around a strange drink. It drugged our elders and the tribal leaders and made them sleep."

I had a bad feeling in my stomach. "Mama, you don't have to tell no more if'n you don't want." I was curious, but I knew this was a hard telling for Mama.

She took my hands in hers. "No, son. You need to know where you come from. And why your Papa and I are working to get our kinsfolk to freedom.

"I was younger than you is now. Just learning to dye cloth and make our Ibo designs in the weaving house. I was drawn to the strangers' colorful clothes, the ruffles on their shirts, and buttons on their breeches. I had never seen these things before.

"One man wanted to trade buttons for our special healing salve. He motioned for me to follow him to the boat." Momma gazed off in the distance as if she was seeing it all again. "When we got to the canoe, he held a cloth over my mouth and nose. I fought to breathe but I was no match for a grown sailor." Mama's tears soaked her handkerchief. "I woke up chained in the belly of a ship with hundreds of others from different tribes. Most talked in other dialects, so we couldn't share our fears and pain. During the long days at sea, when folks was dying all around me, I promised myself I'd stay strong and someday be free to get home."

"Don't cry Mama." I hugged her. "You is so brave. I'd go crazy, if'n I was taken away from you and Papa."

Mama hugged me hard and sniffed. "God took care of me when

I was sold to Massa Dover. I could have gone to a devil of a massa that tortured folks for no reason. But Massa Dover treats us better than most. If'n we get our work done and don't sass the Missus." She pulled away from me and stroked my face. "I met your Papa at Dover Hall. Massa Dover 'lowed us to marry, and soon you came along. You two is my family now. Home is where your family be." Mama wiped away her tears with her apron. "It's gettin' on towards dark. We best be movin' on. Fetch the sweet grass basket, Peter."

I slid the top shut and pulled it out of the water. Four fish were trapped. I had the sudden urge to let them out, to be free. Mama musta knowed what I was thinking.

She put her hand on my shoulder. "Peter, we not like the white massas with no respect for life. Know why we don't eat the she-crabs we find on the beach?"

I shook my head. "Never thought 'bout it. Em and I played with them when we was little."

Mama smiled. "It's 'cause a she-crab lays a million eggs in her lifetime. Some animals are created by God for our provision." She winked at me. "Like these four fish for our fish fry."

Drunkard's Path Pattern

Chapter

As we walked on the path, the shadows grew longer. I noticed a paw print in the damp dirt and squatted for a better look. I put my palm in it. The footprint dwarfed my hand. "Mama, look. A wolf?"

"A bear paw." Mama bent over and traced it with her finger. "We have a quilt pattern, called Bears Paw. We learned it from enslaved Native Americans."

I wiped my muddy hand on my ragged trousers and searched the trees for bears. "Might be best if'n we hurry along."

"Our quilt code pattern looks like this," Mama said. She took a stick and drew a square with four triangles on two sides like bear's claws. "The quilt pattern means 'follow the bear's path'."

Reaching into my pocket for my Ogbe, I shook my head. "I cain't see nothing but danger in tracking a bear."

She motioned me to come along. "When I hang this here quilt on the fence, it means the bears' path will lead runaways to caves where they can hide. These tracks might also help folks find berries or honey, but for sure, water. Bear tracks can keep people from starving, and being thirsty enough to spit cotton."

I walked a little closer to her. "Don't want to come 'cross any bears, Mama."

"The best time to run is in the spring after cold weather. But that be when hungry bears are coming out of hibernation. We gots to stay clear of Creek Indians, patrollers, and bears. They all like to hurt us. But following a bear path may just keep runaways alive."

Secret quilt codes and wagon hidey-holes sure sounded better than doing boring chores all day, every day. The funeral escape was for sure an adventure. But there ain't nothing exciting 'bout Abraham's hanging. Or running from patrollers with tracking dogs. Or following bears to keep from starving.

The more I learned 'bout this business of keeping the secret code, the scarier it got. Life or death scary.

I stroked my Ogbe, praying to the life-giver for protection.

Bear's Paw Pattern

Chapter

On my birthday, I woke to the smell of sizzling bacon and an apple pie baking. Mama was known in these parts for her pies, and apple was my favorite. I hopped out of bed, feeling good 'bout being twelve. Now I'd learn my trade and folks would treat me like a man, not a child.

First thing, after milking, Massa Dover sent word for me to meet him in the library. On my way to the big house I couldn't keep the grin off my face. Massa was sure to tell me I was gonna do carpenter work with Sam starting today.

"Come in and sit down, Peter," Massa Dover told me when I got to the door.

"Yes, sir." I sat on the edge of a red velvet chair. My leg jiggled with excitement. "I is ready to work with Sam now. He's been teaching me how to whittle clothes pins to start me ou—"

"—Peter," Massa Dover interrupted. "I know you're anxious to be a carpenter's apprentice, but I am going to need you to work around the big house a little bit longer. Just until our spring soiree is over. There is much to be done. Besides all the regular chores, there will be cleaning the house top to bottom, sewing our ball clothes, and preparing the meal for fifty folks or more. The young boy who will take over your chores won't be able to keep up. I'm delaying your apprenticeship until after the soiree."

I jumped out of my chair. "But sir! You said when I's twelve. It's my birthday, today. Look at my arm muscles. I's strong, like a man. I's ready to take on big jobs, like carpenter's work."

Massa Dover took off his glasses and pinched the bridge of his nose. "Sorry, son. But sacrifices have to be made for what's best for Dover. Be patient, Peter. You'll have a hammer and nails in your hand soon enough. Now run along and get your work done."

"Yes, sir," I choked out. I mumbled to myself as I trudged down the hall and out the back door. "Why do I have to put off learning a man's job so the big house folks can show off at a big party?" So I went back to my chores like I'd done all my life. Here I was twelve and nothing was different! My grin was long gone.

Em stopped me the next morning on my way to milk Bessie and Mort. "What's wrong, Peter?"

Guess my stomping and grumping gave her a clue. I kept walking. "Your spring ball, fancy pants."

Em hurried to keep up with me. "What are you talking about? You mean the soiree?"

"Yeah. Your daddy won't let me start my training with Sam, 'cause of all the extra work." I jerked the bolt back on the barn door, shoved it open, and grabbed the milk bucket. I led Bessie out of her stall to the milking area and tied her to the post.

Em stroked the cow's leathery hide, then leaned against the barn door and watched me. "You're just tired, Peter."

I plopped down on the three-legged stool. "Tired of nothing changing! Even though I's a man now."

"I say we go out to the beach. Remember how much fun we used to have collecting shells and chasing the crabs?"

I aimed Bessie's udder and squirted Em square in the face. "Don't need no beach. I want to do something different. Not keep cleaning and fetching like a slave boy!"

Em sputtered and coughed, then wiped milk off her face with her sleeve. "But Peter, that's what you are."

I jumped up and kicked the bucket. Milk flew everywhere, soaking into the dirt until nothing was left. My carpenter plans was getting sucked away, just like that milk. Did my hopes have to disappear 'cause I wasn't born rich and white? I stared at Em. "Is that what I am to you, Em?"

Her eyes filled with tears. "Not me, Peter. But that is the way of it around here."

I plopped down hard on the stool and covered my face with my calloused hands. "Why cain't I choose what I want to do?"

Em dropped down on her knees beside me. "I'm sorry I said that Peter." We touched foreheads, like when we was little. "I didn't mean it the way it came out. That's what others think. But I see you for who you are—my brother. Forgive me?"

I pulled away, trying to stay mad. "Go away, Em. I got so much work, I ain't never gonna get done." I went back to milking. The rhythm of the creamy white liquid squirting in the empty metal bucket soothed me some.

Em licked some lingering milk drops off her lips. "'Member that time when Daddy let you go to the beach with me?"

"You forget, I was totin' your picnic stuff." I searched her seaweed-colored eyes. "I remember what happened when he caught us fishing!"

Em shrugged. "Told us to get back to work. That's what he says to everyone. You've been working hard. Come on, Peter." Em winked. "It'll be my birthday present to you, if Daddy asks." She skipped out of the barn.

While I finished up milking, I thought 'bout how everything seemed better when Em was around. Then 'bout Massa putting off my apprenticeship. My temper flared again. It's my birthday, I thought. I've earned some free time! Especially after the way Massa loaded me up with extra chores. I chewed my lip, as I led Bessie back out to graze. Since I run 'round Dover Hall every day, it'd more'n likely take Overseer John a while to figure out I was missing. Nobody pays any mind to the boy who fetches stuff.

I hurried to meet Em on the beach. We had a competition to see who could collect the most shells in our sweet grass baskets. Then we splashed in the waves and made sandcastles. Just like old times. As we sat on the beach, drying out, I threw sand at a crab scurrying by. But 'membering Mama's story, I let it go. Em drew pictures in the sand with a stick. She liked to draw. I watched her. "Em, why is Massa against us being together?"

She looked up and squinted into the sun. "Guess Daddy thinks now that we are almost grown, we can't be friends."

"But you is like the sister I never had." I dug out the moat around our sandcastle with a flat shell. "Why can't things be like they used to be?"

"Guess it's the South Carolina way of it." Em looked up at me with flooded green eyes. "You are supposed to be slavin' and I'm supposed to be bossin'. I just want to stay friends." I scooted over and took her hand. We both sat quiet, listening to the waves and watching the seagulls circle. Em faced me. "Peter, let's swear that we'll always be friends. No matter what." She spit in her palm. I done the same. Then we shook on it. "Repeat after me. I do swear to be forever friends, whatever happens." She was fighting to keep a serious face.

My grin was back. "I sure do swear to always and forever be friends with Em...unless she tries to boss me." Em stuck her tongue out at me. I ran, laughing and splashing into the water. Em was right behind me.

Chapter 10

All spring, Papa led groups of runaways to safe houses on the Underground, and each time, I begged to go. Papa kept saying, "Son, you got three more quilt codes to learn."

Mama and I had no time to talk 'bout quilt codes in the sewing parlor or the grape arbor or anywhere else. All the big house help worked from 'cain't see to cain't see', making fancy dresses and ruffled petticoats for Em and the Missus. That didn't count the trousers, shirts, and waistcoats for Massa Dover. Balls was held at all the big plantations twice a year, spring and fall. 'Cause folks traveled from far away, balls sometimes lasted for a week.

Stitching layers of petticoats, sewing the silk and taffeta dresses, and then topping them off with handmade lace and embroidery was slow, tedious work. Then there was the puffy sleeves with pearl buttons and beaded necklines. Those took hours of hand stitching until our fingers ached. I helped Mama as much as I could. I sewed on buttons, tacked down the lace on the full skirts, and kept the needles threaded. All while daydreaming 'bout building a canoe with Sam. Folks treated me just the same 'cause they saw me doing the same chores. No one seemed to 'member I was twelve now. I hoped Massa Dover didn't forget 'bout me wanting to be a carpenter. My restless returned. I felt like a caged bear.

One cool evening, Papa was working over night at another plantation. Our cabin was 'bout equal distance 'tween the slave quarter and the big house. The cricket and frog sounds were soothing. Mama settled herself in the creaky rocking chair Sam had made for her 'fore I was born. I plopped down on the steps with my knife and a chunk of wood. Sam had told me to keep practicing while I was waitin' to be a carpenter.

Mama pulled a quilt block out of her sewing basket. She held it up and said in a low voice, "Now that we is alone, Peter, let me tell you 'bout another quilt code. This here is the Bow Tie pattern. With the new Fugitive Slave Act working 'gainst us, its message is even more important."

I stopped whittling. "What's that law got to do with this here quilt?"

"After Papa drops off folks at a safe house, other conductors gotta keep moving the group 'long between stations closer to the Mason Dixon Line."

"What's the Mason Dixon Line?" I asked.

Mama took my knife and slashed it through the air, like she was slicing the full moon in half. "It ain't a line you can see. But it's like cutting the country 'cross the middle. The top half is the free states and the bottom half is the slave holding states. Used to be, if we got our kinsmen 'cross the River Jordan, they was safe. Not free yet, but safe 'till they could get some free papers. But with the new law, patrollers can kidnap them in the free north states and drag them back to their owners. Runaways now have to go farther north. Clear to Canada."

"Canada touches the northern states?" I 'membered a map on Massa's desk the day I was called into the library, but I was so mad 'bout not being allowed to start working with Sam, I paid it no mind. Wish Em could sneak me in and let me take a peek at it again.

Mama handed back my whittling knife. "Yes, so now there is no safe states for our people." Mama sighed and stroked the Bow Tie quilt block. "But the best place to hide is sometimes in plain sight."

"You mean like the secret code quilts in our cabin?" I winked. "And on the beds in the big house?"

"You got that right, son." Mama smiled. "The Bow Tie pattern says when runaways get close to the free states, a conductor will give them nice clothes." Mama leaned forward. "It means the group is to wash up, change out of their ragged slave clothes into the clean fancy clothes. They need to hold their heads high and look people in the eye as they stroll through town. If'n they act like they is free blacks, they won't be stopped and asked for their free papers."

"Does that work?" I asked.

"Most times. 'Fore this new Fugitive Slave Act. Now station masters and conductors is gonna need extra clothes for our kinsmen to travel through more free towns to get to Canada. They gots to keep up the disguise of being free blacks, longer. Which is mighty risky."

"Mama, I could make extra sets of breeches and shirts. Papa could have the runaways pass them on up to conductors in the north."

Mama hugged me. "You got big ideas, son. God will provide. But right now you got to help me finish this here Bow Tie quilt."

I laid aside my whittling stick. "Mama, if'n the Missus asks me the name of this pattern, what do I say?"

"You tell her it's the Broken Dishes pattern." She handed me some cut cloth pieces. "Think ahead, Peter. To do our freedom work, you gots to have a ready answer."

I picked up the needle and went to work.

Bow Tie Pattern

Chapter 11

The next day, after I filled the wood bins downstairs, I hauled wood upstairs to the bedroom fireplaces. Rounding a corner I bumped into Em. Firewood scattered across the floor. "Sorry, Em! Didn't see you there." I bent down to pick up the sticks.

She squatted down next to me to help. "Hey, Peter. You been doing any fishing, or beach combing, lately?"

I held out my arms as she stacked on the last pieces of firewood. Em's cat-like eyes sparkled. I knew that look. Most times it meant trouble for me. "Don't know what you is talking 'bout, Miss Emily." I felt strange calling her that. I leaned in and whispered, "Shut yo mouth, girl. Word could get back to Overseer or Massa." At that moment, Sarie passed by. She shook her head and clucked her tongue at us, like when we was little and got caught doing something we wasn't supposed to.

We both stood up at the same time. I yanked one of Em's curls. "You know I'm not 'posed to be talkin' to you, Miss Emily." I stepped past her and walked into her bedroom to unload the wood into the firewood box.

She followed me. "Oh, phewy! Peter, it's me." She crossed her arms. "Stop calling me Miss Emily. Where have you been? Haven't seen you around much."

I froze. Did she know about the secret quilt codes? "Uh, nothing. Just doing extra chores. You know, gettin' ready for the ball." I finished stacking the wood in the wood box and turned around to leave. She was sitting on the narrow daybed at the foot of her pink canopied, feather bed. And there was the Wagon Wheel quilt, spread out as big as daylight. I tried to make my face blank, but Em could read me like one of her books.

She pointed a finger at me. "I know you, Peter Farrow. You're hiding something. Tell me!"

Mama's voice echoed in my head; always have a ready answer. "I..uh...was just curious 'bout something." I had to tell her a truth, 'cause she'd guess what I was thinking, like Mama.

"What? Spit it out!" Em demanded.

"I...I sure would like to have a look-see at that map Massa's got in the library."

"Is that all? Come on. I'll show you now. Daddy's gone to town." Em hurried out the door. "You're with me, so quit worrying."

I followed her down the staircase. "That's what worries me most. Being with you." The main hall was empty. The library was just inside the front doors. It had tall, oak bookcases on three walls with a massive, wood desk in the middle of the room. Probably Sam's work. I ran my hand along the fireplace mantle feeling the cool, smooth, white marble. I hadn't paid no mind 'bout this room the day Massa took away my carpenter training. My bugged-out eyes stared back at me from the mirror over the fireplace. "Look at all them books. You read all these, Em?"

"Some," she said. "But most are boring. About laws and history." Em walked behind the desk and plopped down in Massa Dover's leather chair. She shoved some papers to the side. "Come around here, Peter. The map is under glass on Daddy's desk."

I stood beside her and ran my hand across the glass. "This is God's view of our country?"

"Well, I never thought about what it looked like from heaven, but I guess it is." Em pointed to South Carolina. "This is where we live. Dover Hall is here, a little ways from Charleston."

I squinted. "Have you ever heard of the Mason Dixon Line, Em?"

"It's not a real line, but it might be marked here." We both bent over the map. Emily pointed. "There. It's this dashed line that runs along the Kentucky-Ohio River. See it?"

"Yeah." I traced the snaky line above Missouri, Kentucky and Virginia. "Now where's Canada?" I clamped my mouth shut. Was I asking too many questions? I searched Em's face, but she pointed to the map, like she was my teacher.

"Here it is." She tapped the glass. "When Daddy takes us north during skeeter time, we never go as far as Canada. I would like to see it someday." She chatted away, easy as a summer breeze. I listened, but couldn't help noticing how far it was from South Carolina to Canada.

The sound of heavy boots in the hallway made us both jump. Overseer John burst into the library so fast I just had time to straighten up and take a step back. "What in the sam-hill is going on in here?" His face looked like a thunderstorm about to break.

"Sir, I was just...uh,...uh, leaving." I tried to run past him, but he blocked the door.

Em shrugged. "Peter and I was looking at the map. We used to have lessons together when we was little. He was just curious."

"Miss Emily, you seem to forget Peter is a slave. Not your kin." Overseer John grabbed my arm. "I'll make sure Peter remembers next time." Overseer pulled me into the hall and snarled, "Slaves don't have no need of maps, 'cause they got no place to go."

Em ran to Overseer and pulled on his shirt sleeve. "Daddy will be here any minute," she huffed. "Peter and I are friends. Daddy knows this."

"You stay put, little Miss." He shoved her back into the library and slammed the big oak door shut. He pulled out a ring of keys and locked Em inside. I could hear her pounding on the door and yelling my name. I made a run for it, but Overseer caught me and shoved me down the hall, out the front door and straight into one of the massive marble pillars.

I bounced back into him like a ball and he whirled me around to face him. Pain shot through my brain. Dazed, I choked back a mouthful of vomit. I rubbed the bump that was popping out on my head. "I meant no harm, sir. Just looking."

"Curious about maps, are you?" Overseer John grabbed my shirt and pulled me in close. He was missing a few teeth and his tobacco breath gagged me. "You getting ideas, boy? Ideas about running? I'll beat that outa of you." He reached for his whip on his belt.

I squirmed, trying to break free. Pictures of Sam's bloody back flashed in my mind.

"Stop!" Massa Dover came riding up from behind the hedges and flower gardens that surrounded the circle drive. "What's the problem here?"

"Caught this one hanging around Miss Emily in your library, sir." Overseer John shook me like a rag doll. "First, he interrupts me whipping Sam, and now he's snooping 'round maps. Seems to me he's getting too big for his britches. I was about to take him down a few notches, so he doesn't forget his place."

Massa mounted the marble steps. "I'll handle this, John."

Overseer let me go. "Yes, sir." He gritted his teeth but stepped back. "You need me, I'll be close by."

Massa put his hand under my chin and forced me to look up at him. "Why were you in the library, Peter?"

"I missed doing lessons with Em, uh Miss Emily, like when we was little. Wanted to learn more stuff."

Massa took a breath and let it out real slow. "Peter, I overlooked you protecting Sam from a beating the other day, because I know you got a soft heart. I let it slide when I found you and Emily dancing under the willow tree. I know you two grew up here like brother and sister. But now that you're older, I can't allow you any special treatment." He ran his fingers through his graying hair. "Your family lives in the best cabin away from the quarters. I let your Papa hire out his blacksmith work. Your mother helps out at the Butler hospital, because she has a gift for healing. I don't take their earnings like other owners would."

I nodded, tears of relief running down my cheeks.

Massa stepped back, but wagged a finger in my face. "I'm warning you, now, son. If I catch you taking advantage of my kindness again, I'll be forced to take action." I rubbed the Ogbe in my pocket. My shoulders sagged in relief. Thank goodness he never found out 'bout our day at the beach! "You understand me?" Massa asked. I nodded, wiping snot with my shirt sleeve. "As soon as our spring soiree is over, I still plan for you to be an apprentice to Sam. Don't mess that up. You'll have no reason to be around Emily anymore. Those days are over, Peter. Now get to your chores and stay in your place."

"Yes, sir." I ran like the wind out of there.

Chapter 12

The next few days, I was so scared, I 'bout broke my neck looking over my shoulders. Overseer seemed to be everywhere. Most times sitting on his horse staring at me from the trees. Sometimes he'd ride up close to where I was milking or picking strawberries and just miss me with his tobacco spit. Other times I'd hear the clip-clop of his horse behind me. I'd slow my steps and take a peek behind me. He'd stop a ways back, but he'd be curling and uncurling his whip 'round his arm. I stayed ahead of my chores. I didn't want to take no chances. I kept my Ogbe with me, and some days even carried it in my shirt pocket to be close to my heart.

Soon as I got my everyday work done, I high-tailed it to the sewing parlor. If'n we was alone, Mama and I sewed extra clothes to send north, or we worked on the Bow Tie Quilt. When other enslaved ladies was with us, we worked on the fancy clothes for the ball. I never told Mama or Papa 'bout Em and me getting caught in the library. Only harm done was to my head. And my hurt feelings.

As soon as we finished sewing the fancy clothes, it was time to do extra cleaning and polishing to make the downstairs shine. The morning before the Ball, Cook started in on the pie making. I had to hustle to get the apples and peaches picked for her baking. After milking Bessie and Mort, and carrying the buckets to the dairy, I toted crocks of cream, butter and milk to Cook and her helpers. They was elbow deep in dough for bread and pie crusts. When that was done, I joined the other big house help on the main floor.

Cleaning seemed to never end. We polished candle sticks, silverware, the marble fireplace mantles, ivory-framed mirrors including all the furniture, the pictures and the statues under the dome. Across the front hall from the library was the ladies' parlor. On the same side was the men's smoking room at the back of the main hall. We opened the pocket doors separating the two rooms to make one long ballroom running the length of the mansion. We rolled up the heavy carpets and carried them up the twisting staircases to the attic. Then we worked on the wood floors until you could see your reflection in them. Balanced on a tall ladder, I dusted a hundred glass pieces in the crystal chandelier hanging under the skylight. Others moved furniture 'round as the Missus barked orders. Some folks took down the heavy fabric on the floor-to-ceiling windows and replaced them with the sheer, summer hangings to let in the evening breeze.

I was dusting a painting of the Dover family in the front hall when Em sauntered past. "Be careful, Peter. That's an arm-and-a-leg picture."

"Don't be talking to me," I hissed. "You 'bout got me whipped by Overseer."

"I'm sorry, Peter, I tried to stop him, but he locked me in the library." Em chewed her lip. "You did ask to see the map."

I turned back to her. "You should've stopped me. I ain't talking to you."

Em frowned. "I can't believe you're blaming me."

I wiped my rag over the picture and looked close at the painting of Emily with her family. "What you mean this here is an arm-leg picture?"

Em crossed her arms and tapped her foot. "I thought you weren't talking to me, Peter." I gave her my angry side-eye look. Then we both broke out laughing. "Peter, you're too curious for your own good. You really want to know?" she asked.

"Just tell me quick, 'fore someone sees us." I jumped off the ladder and pulled her 'round the corner into the ballroom. We squatted down behind the S-shaped courting couch that kept unmarried couples from sitting close. It felt like we was playing hide and seek again.

Em whispered. "Mother and Daddy usually go to the painter's studio and pick out bodies that have already been painted. Then the artist has us sit while he paints on our heads and faces. It doesn't cost as much." She giggled at my raised eyebrows. "But on that picture you were dusting, the artist painted our whole real bodies. That's why it's called an arm-and-a-leg picture and it cost lots more money."

I grinned. "You tellin' me that painting cost so much you have to sell off an arm and a leg to pay for it?" We both laughed out loud. Then we peeked over the couch to see if anyone heard us. "Really Em, painting bodies without heads is creepy. Guess rich folks got money to do strange things, though." I stretched out my legs and rested my back against the couch.

Emily leaned in and whispered. "You want to see some crazy rich folks? Sneak in tonight during the ball, ...uh...spring soiree, and you'll see folks showing off for sure."

Just then Sarie came looking for me. "Peter? Where is you, boy?" We quick hunkered down. Her footsteps retreated down the hall toward the back porch. "If you can hear me, you get yourself to the cook house. You best not be hiding to get out of work. I'll find you, boy." Her voice faded as the door slammed shut.

"Gotta go, Em." I scrambled back to the ladder. "Sure would like to take a peek at the ball. But I best not. Overseer been watching me real close."

"Peter, you know you want to see it. I'll meet you at the back porch. After our guests finish supper they'll head to the ballroom. In the confusion, no one will even notice." She winked and flashed her I-dare-you grin then marched up the front stairs. That girl could tempt a saint to do wrong!

Chapter 13

I knew I was taking a risk if'n I snuck into the party, but I sure did want to take a peek at the rich folks in all their finery.

As I carried the crystal and china dishes to Will I fretted 'bout whether to meet Em or not. He didn't pay me no mind. He was too busy settin' the table just right, with the lacey cloth, candles and the polished silverware. When carriages started coming, the Missus scolded us to hurry and get dressed in our best black and white clothes. Since I was fetching dishes loaded with food between the cook house and the dining room, I slowed my steps to get a better look.

The Master, the Missus, and Em greeted their guests at the huge double doors. The men tipped their black silk hats while the women curtseyed and offered their gloved hands for kisses. The line of rich folks spilled down the marble steps of the veranda onto the stone pathways wandering through the hedges and the flowerbeds.

After my cookhouse work was done, I showed the surrey drivers 'round back to the carriage house. I unhitched the horses and led them to the stables where I fed and watered them. Some folks would be leaving at daybreak. Ones that lived faraway would likely stay overnight. Others stayed on for days or weeks.

I was jumpy as a grasshopper, waiting for supper to be finished. Instead of helping Will with clearing the table, I snuck 'round the house and hid in the bushes by the back porch. Finally, I heard a rustle of petticoats and there was Em, looking like a princess in her green velvet dress, her emerald eyes sparkling.

I popped up behind her. "Boo!"

She grabbed the railing to steady herself. "Peter, you scared the daylights out of me!" Her mischievous grin returned. "I knew you wouldn't be able to help yourself."

I bounded up the steps. "I cain't stay long. Suppose to be helping ShooFly clean up."

"Follow me." She opened the back door. "Stay in the corner behind this spiral staircase and we can peek between the metal steps into the ballroom."

I stayed in the shadows, tiptoeing behind her hooped skirt. We settled in our hiding spot just as some folks moseyed 'cross the hall from the dining room to the ballroom. I heard the flowing harmonies of the harpsicord piano, a violin, and a stringed harp taller than me.

I'd sewed with Mama for the Dover family since I could 'member, but I'd never seen so many rich-looking clothes in one place in my life. Sparkling jewels, like candles floating on water, were sprinkled 'cross silk skirts and bodices. Jewelry dripped from ears, circled necks, and twinkled in cuff links on the men's stiff shirt sleeves. Most of the ladies had their hair piled up like birds' nests and decorated with flowers and feathers.

Em twisted around to face me in our tight space. "What do you think?"

I stepped back to keep from drowning in her skirt. "I never seen nothing like it in all my days."

"I told you." Em loved showing me new things. "Look! The dancing is starting."

"I wish we could...just get ...a little closer." I edged out from behind her and sprinted across the hall into the opposite dark corner.

The candlelight from the chandeliers bounced between the dancers' dazzling jewelry to the silver embroidered designs on the sheer window hangings, to the gold-trimmed mirrors above the two marble fireplaces. The place was lit up like a harvest moon in a star-studded night sky.

Em grabbed my hands and whispered, "Do the steps like I taught you at the willow tree." We swayed to the music in the shadow of the two back staircases, just like the fancy folks in the parlor. I stepped on Em's feet a few times but she just laughed. The men's long coat tails spiraled when they turned and the women's full dresses spun out when they twirled, like flowers opening in spring. I closed my eyes, soaking it up to 'member forever. Em stopped and jerked me back into the shadows.

But it was too late.

I opened my eyes to see her staring in horror over my shoulder. I spun around and looked into the stone-cold eyes of Overseer John. "Sir, I, I..." Think fast. Where was my ready answer? "I was on my way to help ShooFly clear the supper dishes."

"Looks to me like you were dancing with Miss Emily. You think you're a guest now?" He pasted on a smile and nodded to some folks strolling by. But it didn't hide the anger in his gray eyes. "You know you aren't to be inside the main hall. Ever. Seems you stepped out of your place again, boy."

Em stepped in front of me. "Wait, Mr. John, I asked Peter to come see the party."

He brushed her aside. "This isn't any of your concern, young lady. Peter's twelve. He seems to think he has the run of the place, like white folk. He squeezed my shoulder so hard it almost brought me to my knees. He steered me out the back door. Even before we got down the back steps, he started in on me. "I warned you to stay in your place or you'd get some of what Sam got the other day."

I wiggled and tried to pry loose from his vise-like grip. "I know, sir. I was just taking a look-see at the fancy clothes Mama and I worked on these past weeks. I was just 'bout to leave."

Overseer's grip tightened. "Don't got my whip on me, but I'll come find you in the quarter. Your back will be in shreds when I..."

Em burst out the back door, pulling Massa Dover with her down the steps. He stopped in front of us and held one arm out to keep Em back. He looked hard at Overseer. "Let him go, John. I'll take it from here."

Overseer let go but stayed next to me. "With all due respect sir, this boy has twice before got out of line. I was about to teach..." Massa Dover raised his hands, palms out. Overseer John shut his mouth and stepped back.

Massa looked at me with disappointment in his eyes. "Peter, I thought we had an understanding. This is how you thank me? By disobeying?" He lowered his voice. "Why do you keep breaking the rules? I know you're full of spirit. I know you and Emily are close. But your world is miles apart from hers. And always will be. When boundaries are crossed between masters and enslaved people, there are consequences. Always."

Hysterical, Em ran to her father. "Papa don't. This is Peter! He taught me to make mud pies and skip rocks and climb trees and put fishing worms on my hook. Peter was my school mate during tutoring. He's like a brother to me. We were just having fun, like we used to do. He was just curious. We didn't do no harm."

Overseer stepped closer. "Master Dover, other slaves are taking note of his privileges. This isn't his first 'mistake'. He interfered with Sam's whipping, then I caught him in the library with Emily, and now he's dancing at your ball? What will your guests think?"

Massa got down on one knee and stared deep into my soul. I could see the hurt in his eyes. "Peter, why?"

I tore my eyes away and looked at my feet. "Sir, I don't understand. Em and I got different skin colors but that don't bother us. We was raised like family." I frowned. "What's changed?"

Massa put his hands on my shoulders. Was he was going to give me another talking to and then let me go? "I'll tell you what's changed. You're almost grown. I looked the other way when you and Emily were little. But now I can't reign you back in. You think like a free white, but your body is an enslaved black man-child. You give me no choice. I'll sell you at the Charleston slave auction next Saturday." He let go of me and stood up. Massa turned to Overseer John. "Go tell Peter's folks he'll be sold in a week." Overseer sneered at me and walked away.

Emily screamed, "No!" She covered her face with her gloved hands.

I went limp. I surely didn't hear right. My ears was ringing. I stared at him. "What? Sir, what'd you say?"

"I'm selling you Peter." Massa Dover looked away but I thought I saw his blue eyes glisten with tears. "It's my fault for letting you and Em grow up like brother and sister. Now that you're both older, it has to change. It's too late. I can see that it's never going to be different."

I sunk to my knees, fumbling for my Ogbe. "What 'bout Mama and Papa?"

"Oh, they're staying. They're too valuable to me." He pulled at his stiff-collared shirt and straightened his waistcoat. "Just you." He grabbed Emily's arm and dragged her back to the house. Em cried out, looking over her shoulder and reaching out for me.

I stayed on my knees and crawled after them. "Sir, Massa, please," my voice croaked. "Please have mercy on me. I'll take a whipping from Overseer. Don't take me away from my family," I begged. "I'll do anything. I'll give up on being a carpenter and work every day in the cotton."

Massa never looked back. But his shoulders slumped as he disappeared through the back door, pulling Em along with him. When the door slammed shut, I gathered my strength and ran to our cabin, just in time to see Overseer John telling my parents what happened.

Overseer leered at me. "You got what you deserved, boy. The masters down south will beat the high-and-mighty out of you." He turned and strolled back to the big house. I slumped face down into the grass like a slaughtered animal.

Chapter 14

I don't know how long Mama held me, crying and rocking. My head buzzed trying to think how to change Massa Dover's mind. Papa helped me into the cabin, the only home I'd ever known. Then he left to go talk some sense into Massa.

I woke up sometime in the middle of the night with Scout curled up beside me. Mama and Papa huddled by the fireplace talking low. Papa whittled fast, wood chips flying all over. "Massa ain't gonna change his mind. We cain't let Peter be sold down south."

Mama's rocking chair was doing double time. Her eyes was glued to her open Bible. "I heard tell the massas' down south work folks hard. Most don't last long." She ran her hands over the scripture pages as if searching for the answer. "What we gonna do?"

Silence. Just the creak of the rocker and the scrape of the whittling knife. Then Papa faced Mama and talked low and serious-like. I couldn't make it out over the creaking rocker, but I could see Mama's eyes widen. "What you saying?" Papa glanced back at the bed. I squeezed my eyes shut. Then he leaned towards her and whispered something.

I opened my eyes a slit, enough to see Papa back to whittling. "If'n Peter is sold down south, we'd likely never find him to buy him back. I'll try again talking Massa out of it. Peter's got to carry on our work someday." I could hear Mama sniffing and rocking, slow this time. They talked real low now and then, but I was too busy crying like a baby into my pillow to pay attention. When I was plumb wore out, I went back to worrying.

What had I done? I had bit my fingernails to nubs and had rubbed my Ogbe so hard a groove was forming in the middle. I had torn my family apart, for sure. Slammed the door on me ever being a secret code keeper like Mamma and Papa. I went back over the last few days in my head. My troubles had started with saving Sam. Then there was fishing with Em, going to the beach with Em, getting caught in the library with Em, and sneaking into the ball with Em.

I tried to make sense of it. Most had to do with me and Em. We was both people. Our skin was different but we had so much more the same. Why did it matter?

I fell asleep wondering how Papa could change Massa's mind. I had dreams of Em and me playing, and nightmares of Papa getting whipped for begging Massa to let me stay. I woke up in a sweat.

Over the next few days, my kinsmen ignored me if Overseer was in sight, like I had a sickness that was catching. I guess folks thought I'd stir up trouble for them too. I told myself, if'n I kept busy and worked hard 'nough, Massa would take notice and give me another chance. I couldn't keep much food down. My hands got the shakes while I was working and I gnawed at my lower lip until it bled. Mama had to put her special salve on it.

Em was nowhere around.

Papa and Mama was acting strange, too. Every morning and every night I'd ask Papa if Massa was 'bout to go back on selling me and let me stay. Papa just shook his head and looked sad. "You let me handle this, Peter. Just keep your head down and get your work done."

I had just come in from washing up and was dead tired. Mama was stirring the soup pot over the fireplace. "Peter, supper ain't done yet. Now you get on out back and dig up some sweet 'tators from our 'tator bank.

"But why, Mama?" I stared at her. "That's our winter stash. For when we cain't hunt."

Mama whipped around with her wooden spoon raised, ready to knock me on the head. "Do as I say! Don't you dare sass me, son."

Another day, I caught Mama packing our secret code quilts. She explained, "Just making sure Overseer don't get them if'n he decides to search our cabin." Mama and Papa did more whispering, even more than when they was planning an escape. They would glance over at me with tears in their eyes. But we never talked 'bout what I would face down south.

As Saturday got closer, the groove in my Ogbe got deeper, 'cause it was in my hand every day. I struggled to fight down panic. I had wild thoughts of running away on my own. I thought I could find my way, even though I ain't never been far from Dover. After all, I knew most of the quilt codes. I was fast. Maybe fast 'nough to outrun the dogs and the patrollers. I knew the odds was stacked against a lone runaway. Most got caught or killed.

Every time I passed Mama or Papa during the day I'd hug them. I wanted to say sorry for what I had done, but I couldn't find the words. Probably 'cause I knowed I didn't do nothin' wrong. I wanted Em to know I didn't blame her but I didn't dare try to find her to tell her.

I wanted to leave something for my family to 'member me by but I had nothing. Then I patted my pocket. My Ogbe? Could I survive the South's cotton fields without my life-giving protection? Papa's words haunted me—"Always keep it with you, son."

As I lay on my corn husk mattress one night, I took out my Ogbe and watched the fire light shine 'cross it's smooth surface. I put my thumb in the middle groove and stroked it, feeling it's warmth and peace. I turned it over in my hands and realized it looked like a tiny canoe from all my rubbing. I knew what I had to do. I kissed my Ogbe and squeezed it one last time. Then I stuffed it into a hole in Mama and Papa's feather mattress. I figured if Massa Dover or Overseer searched our cabin, they'd leave it be. Meant nothing to them. It was my goodbye forever to my family. I wanted to pass on its life-giving peace and protection back to the ones I loved—Mama, Papa and Em.

North Star pattern

Chapter 15

Two days 'fore I was gonna be sold down south, Mama fixed a big supper. It reminded me of the Last Supper in the Bible. Was I 'bout to go to my death?, I wondered. After we ate, Papa held Wednesday evening prayer service like usual. But there were so many folks that night they spilled outside the grape arbor.

By the time a thunderstorm rolled in, I was feeling poorly. Probably sick from fear, or shame for not getting to be a secret code keeper. At the end of the meeting, Papa stood me at the back so my kinsmen could say goodbye. Folks laid hands on me and prayed. Some hugged so tight I could barely breathe. Others looked me in the eye and dissolved into tears. I crumpled to my knees, begging God to save me.

The next thing I knew, I woke up in blackness. Out of habit, I reached for my Ogbe. It wasn't there. Was I dead? Was I in Abraham's coffin? I was on my stomach and couldn't move, but the jostling told me wherever I was, I was moving. When my fingers found the breathing holes, I knew I was in the false bottom of Papa's wagon. But why? How? My head hurt too much to figure it out. I peeked out one of the holes and watched the ground pass by. But I was so sleepy, I dozed off again.

I woke up again kicking and screaming. Maybe I'd already been sold and Massa had Papa haul me down south. But I wasn't in chains.

My head still ached, though. Finally, the wagon stopped.

Papa and Sam pulled me out of the hidey-hole. My legs was too trembly to stand. They laid me out on the top of the wagon like a feed sack. I took big gulps of the cool night air to clear the cobwebs in my mind. "What happened?" I asked.

The wagon started rolling again and Mama scrambled from the wagon seat to sit by me. "I'm sorry, Peter. I had to give you my sleeping potion at supper. We had to keep it secret—to get you out of Dover. You been asleep for two days."

I grabbed her hand, too dizzy to sit up. "We is going to freedom land?"

Mama patted my leg, and a ghost of a smile touched her lips. "We is."

Papa turned 'round in the wagon seat. "Liza, I believe that storm was a sign of God's protection. The rain has washed away our footprints and wagon tracks. And tThe thunder covered our noises through the underbrush."

Scout jumped up on the wagon next to me. Mama crawled back to her seat next to Papa. I stroked Scout's back feeling calm for the first time in a long while. I listened to the hoot owls and bull frogs.

Sam jumped onto the wagon and sat beside me, laying his carved walking stick 'tween us. The night sky was blanketed in stars, and 'cause of the full moon, I could see runaways was walking behind the wagon. I sat up. "Where did these folks come from?"

Sam turned to me. "We picked up some kinsmen 'long the way. Even though we did our best to keep it secret, a few from Dover got wind of a group leaving. I think they was worried Massa was needing money and might sell them too." Sam told me how Papa and Mama had to hurry our run, since Massa Dover was as stubborn as a mule and was dead set on selling me. They drugged me to make sure I wouldn't let it slip to Emily. They couldn't take a chance of Overseer getting wind of it. Sam patted my leg. "You gonna be fine. Your folks would do anything to save you. Your papa, being a monkey wrench, heard 'bout other enslaved folks nearby who was desperate to get away, so he routed our escape to pass by and pick them up. That's how we ended up with this crowd of fifteen runaways."

Mama scooted to the back of the wagon. "You feeling okay, son?

Your head will clear soon. Takes a few days."

Tears filled my eyes. "Mama, I's sorry for bringing this trouble down on us." I was exhausted and frustrated. I lay back again and stared up into the sky. "I wanted to be a secret code keeper and help you and Papa."

Mama smiled sadly. "Peter, Papa and I will always be doing freedom work." She lay down next to me, searching the sky. "I didn't get to teach you the last quilt codes."

"Which ones?" I asked.

Mama pointed to the star-sprinkled sky. "See the Big Dipper? Nights like this one is the best time for running. That's when conductors move runaways through the Underground. If'n you is ever running alone, follow the North Star. That's what the star-patterned quilt is saying. Find the Big Dipper and trace its handle towards the bright North Star."

"What do we follow if'n we is running in daylight?"

"Misty, rainy days are best," she said. "Keep off the main paths in the woods. Closer you is to the North, the safer it is to travel by day. If'n you have to run in the day, follow the geese and you won't lose your way."

She and Papa had got many folks to freedom using these quilt codes. They would take these codes to their grave, just passing down the secrets to a trusted few, like Sam and me.

Were my hopes of being a code keeper gone forever?

Would the codes be forgotten 'cause of me?

"What is the last pattern, Mama?"

"It's the Flying Geese pattern. Geese fly north in the spring. We has to run then, 'cause we got no warm clothes for the cold weather. If'n you get lost day or night, look to the sky. God will give you signs."

I looked over at Mama, the stars reflecting in her eyes. "Why you telling me this now? I ain't never gonna be a secret code keeper. We all going be in freedom land together. After this run, we won't be needing the quilt codes no more."

Mama kept her eyes on the sky. "Life always be changing, son. You never know when you might be on your own and these codes will save you."

"What you saying, Mama?" My neck hairs stood up on alert.

I looked 'round. It was quiet, too quiet. No crickets. No hoot owl calls. Only sound was our kinsmen tromping behind the wagon in a scattered line.

Flying Geese pattern

Chapter 16

A faraway sound became yelps, whines, barks...something crashing through the woods. Dogs? Tracking dogs? But Papa said the storm gave us a head start? What happened? How did the patrollers track us so soon? Overseer John must have come looking for me, ransacked the cabin, and then let the dogs smell the scent from our clothes. Mama climbed back into the wagon seat and said, "Dogs coming!"

Scout whined and jumped off the wagon. Papa jerked Hampton and Mamie to a stop. "Scout knows. He's warned me many times." Papa stood up, cupped his hands 'round his mouth, and made a great horned owl call—our danger signal. "Whooo, whooo."

The straggling runaways looked to the wagon. Papa waved his arms motioning folks to come closer. He flicked the reins, and the horses took off for the riverbank. When the wagon came to a stop, Papa jumped down. "Peter! Sam! Help me unhitch the team from the wagon." I jumped down, but my fingers fumbled with the harness. Sam and Papa's hands were strong and steady. "Tie the horses in that grove of trees." I grabbed the reins from Papa.

When the first runners caught up to us, Papa said, "Patrollers are tracking us! Help me back the wagon into this cave. I'll stay here and stall them." He turned to Mama. "Liza, get the runaways 'cross the river!"

At the riverbank, Mama motioned for our kinsfolk to swim to the other side. A mother with her baby swaddled on her back, broke away from the group and grabbed Mama's arm. "I can't swim."

Mama put her finger on the woman's lips. "Shush! Stay calm." Then she turned to me. "Bring Mamie and Hampton down to the river. They is going to help this woman and her young'un get 'cross." Mama turned back to the sobbing woman. "Calm down. Our horses will swim you and your baby to the other side."

The frightened woman shook her head and took a step back. "Oh Lordy, no! I cain't..."

I guided Hampton and Mamie to the water. Other folks was splashing and running past us. Mama touched the woman's arm. "Trust me now. You got to do this to save your young'un! You got no choice." The woman stepped into the water and clung to Mama. "Hold on to the horse's tail, and float on your stomach."

I knowed this was something I could do. "Mama, Sam and I'll get her 'cross and take care of the horses on the other side." Mama nodded to us. Sam took the reins. The woman was shaking so hard, I prayed she wouldn't lose her grip on Hampton's tail. I held on to Mamie's tail and swam beside her.

Sam talked her through it. "Kick your feet and hold your head up. Let the horses do the work. When you feel the current pulling, just drift, but **don't let go.**"

Papa ran to the river's edge and yelled to us. "Peter, you and Sam stay over on the far bank and help folks hide. Then send the horses back 'cross the river. If the patrollers find our wagon, they'll wonder where the horses is." The crowd behind him rushed toward the river. He turned back to them, hands raised. "Listen to me," he said trying to calm the group." They stopped but it was like holding back a stampede. I strained my ears to hear his instructions. His voice was low but firm. "Let the current float you down a ways before climbing out on t'other side. That away the dogs can't find your scent. Then get away from the riverbank. Hide wherever you can. Up in the trees, inside logs, back in caves or deep in the underbrush. Stay out of sight. I'll come for ya when they is gone." The tracking dogs barked in the distance. The restless runaways surged forward into the dark water. Papa raised his voice to be heard. "Stay hid 'til you hear me whistling. Help each other, now."

Thundering hooves could be heard in the distance. I prayed under my breath, "God save us." As the last of the group disappeared downstream, I helped the woman and her whimpering baby out of the water. I circled Hampton and Mamie 'round and led them back into the river. The moon was bright and I could see Papa picking up sticks. What's he doing? Building a fire? That'll lead them right to us!

Mama was the last to swim across. Sam took her hand and helped her up the riverbank. We both turned to see Papa starting a fire. I slapped the horse's flanks and they swam back across. The barking, snarling dogs seemed real close. I was trembling. Not sure if it was the cool night air on my wet clothes or fear for Papa facing the patrollers alone. "I can't leave him over there, Mama. I's going stay with him."

Mama kissed me on the forehead. "Go on, Peter. Sam and I'll see after the others." They hurried into the tree line. "We'll be watching over you from the woods."

I jumped into the water and stumbled out on the other side behind the horses. I grabbed their reins and re-tied them in the grove. Papa jumped up from the small fire. "Peter! What are you...?" A twig snapped! Terrified, we turned expecting to face a man-eating dog or a slave hunter on horseback. It was only a skunk. Papa whispered, "Thank you, Jesus."

I froze. "If'n we don't move, the skunk will mosey on by. Right, Papa?"

"Yeah, but I heard 'bout a trick from a fellow monkey wrench." He held out his arm to block my path. "Step back." And then he ran straight at the skunk. When it lifted its tail, Papa twisted so that the nose-burning spray hit his back. Only a sprinkle hit me but the horrible stench caused tears to pour down my face. Papa's face was red, his nose was dripping, and his eyes was running.

As soon as the skunk lumbered off into the woods, I said, "You lost your mind?"

"Watch." Papa pulled off his shirt and drug it through the dirt where our group had crossed. "We cain't let the patrollers know runaways came this way. Get your shirt off and do what I do." I watched Papa swishing his shirt in the mud along the riverbank making the footprints disappear. I took off my shirt and followed behind, wiping out our set of footprints.

"Peter, the skunk smell will burn the bloodhounds' noses and throw them off our scent." Papa dipped his shirt in the water. "We spread out our wet shirts on the bushes at the cave entrance to discourage the slave hunters from finding the wagon. Scout whimpered, but he followed at our heels in spite of our stink.

Chapter 17

"Peter, build up the fire," said Papa. I coaxed the smoldering flame to life with twigs while Papa grabbed travel blankets and dumped them next to the fire, between the cave and the riverbank. "Roll up in this and act like you is sleeping. Don't say nothing."

Dogs and men carrying torches broke through the trees. Papa and I closed our eyes, just as the horses galloped into the clearing. I laid real still taking deep breaths like I was sleeping. I missed my Ogbe so bad it hurt. The men circled us. I heard Papa say, "What? What is it?"

I cracked open one eye and saw him blink against the torch light. The dogs sniffed and whined all 'round us. I sat up stretching and yawning. A man with a nasty-looking whip seemed to be the boss man. "Grab them!" Two of the patrollers jumped from their saddles and ran towards us.

But when they caught the skunk smell, they backtracked.

"Son of a rattler!" choked out a squat man with a ratty beard 'tween coughing spells.

A bald man whipped his head 'round looking every which way. "Holy hallelujah! Where's the blasted skunk?" Both men pulled up their grimy neck scarves and covered all but their eyes. They kicked their way through the confused dogs. Ratty Beard jerked me to my feet. He pinned my arms behind my back. Baldie grabbed Papa.

Papa struggled to pull free. "Hold on now. I's Massa Thomas Dover's blacksmith from Dover Hall. Massa is trading out some work, so I is going to the Shelton Plantation up yonder. There be lots of metalwork so my son came 'long to help." The men looked us over like hungry bears. I swallowed hard and waited. Scout growled. He stood between us and the horses while the tracking dogs circled and whined, tails 'tween their legs.

Bossman spit tobacco at my feet. "Prove it." Baldie let go of Papa but stayed next to him.

Papa fumbled with the chain 'round his neck, buying time. "I got my slave tag right here. You fellas hunting runaways?"

Ratty Beard poked me in the ribs with the butt of his gun. "Hurry up, or I'll make your son sorry!" I bent over trying to breathe. Vomit filled my mouth. I spit it out.

Papa held up the metal square with his name engraved on it. "Here. Here it is."

Bossman grabbed a torch and moved in closer to read the words out loud. "Dover Hall, Peter Farrow, Sr., South Carolina."

Anger rolled off both Ratty Beard and Baldie. I was certain they wanted to claim we was runaways and collect the bounty. But after a signal from Bossman, they stepped away, mumbling behind their neck scarves. Bossman slammed the whip back in his saddlebag. "You see any runaways come this way?"

Papa shook his head. "No sir. Been sleeping." He pointed to our blankets and the flickering fire.

Ratty Beard walked towards the cave. "That there your wagon?"

"Yes, sir. For my 'smithing tools and supplies."

I pointed to Hampton and Mamie in the grove of trees. "Horses over there." I realized too late the pair was still harnessed, wet and breathing hard, a clue they had made a quick trip 'cross the river.

Ratty Beard ignored me and looked to Bossman. "Want us to search the wagon?"

Papa shuffled his feet; a sure sign he was worried they'd find the hidey hole. Bossman's horse sidestepped, sensing his rider's frustration. "Nah, there ain't enough room to hide fifteen runaways in that wagon."

I worked to keep my face blank, but I was smiling like a fool on the inside.

Bossman kicked out at the whining dogs crowded 'round the horses. They stayed clear of the skunk-scented riverbank. His stallion pranced in a circle. "Worthless dogs! The skunk throwed them off scent. Let's go, men. Gotta keep moving. Got more hunting to do." Baldie and Ratty Beard mounted up and whipped their horses into a run.

When the men was out of sight, Papa reached into his pocket and threw a handful of Mama's hush puppies to the dogs at the back of the pack.

"What you doing, Papa?" I reached out to snatch one back, as a dog came running for it. "We need these for us."

Papa yanked my arm back. "Got Mama's sleeping herbs mixed in them. These tracking dogs 'bout to be knocked out cold. Just like you was in the wagon."

I smiled. "Is that why these is called hush puppies?" Papa nodded and relaxed. The dogs ate them right up then trotted after the horses and the other bloodhounds. Papa squatted down and added sticks to the fire. I collapsed on the ground, mopping my forehead with the corner of my blanket. Scout paced between the fire and the cave. The patrollers had to be close.

Papa winked at me and said, loudly, "Get some shut eye, boy. Early day tomorrow."

I lay down but I was fidgety. Scout sensed my restless and curled up next to me. It soothed me some. I looked 'cross the river wondering how Mama and Sam was gonna sleep in a tree. I didn't know much 'bout running but I figured it was best for all of us to stay put at least for the night, in case the patrollers decided to circle back. I watched the flickering flames until I dozed off.

Felt like I had just shut my eyes when Papa shook me awake. It was still dark. "Peter, they's gone. Get up. We gotta find our folks." Papa hitched Hampton and Mamie to the wagon, while I kicked dirt over the fire pit and rolled up our blankets.

As soon as we got the wagon 'cross the river t'other side, Mama and Sam come running. Mama squeezed me so hard, I squealed. "You okay, Peter?" Mama pulled up my shirt. I flinched when she ran her fingers over my ribs. "I saw that nasty man hit you with his gun. Feels like nothing is broke, though." She pulled my shirt down. "You 'll be fine. Just mighty sore for a while."

Sam came up and ruffed up my hair. "Peter, I is proud the way you stayed calm when the patrollers tried to break you down."

Papa drove Hampton and Mamie up and down beside the river, while Sam and I whistled to give folks the all-clear signal. We gathered some but others was hid deeper back in the trees away from the river. We crisscrossed through the woods for hours. Papa wouldn't leave until we rounded up all fifteen of our group. That was the kind of conductor he was.

I'd never get the chance to find out what kind of conductor I might be.

Chapter 18

We got to the "station" as the sun peeked over the hills. Papa pulled the wagon into a covered shed behind the barn. I never been so glad to lay eyes on an old quilt. The Log Cabin quilt with the red square was hanging on the fence, fluttering in the breeze. The conductors was white folks that went by Gramps and Gram. Mama told me later they was Quakers, a religion that didn't believe in slavery. They was 'fraid we had been caught 'cause we was so late getting here.

As Gramps helped Papa unhitch the wagon and wipe down Mamie and Hamp, we told him 'bout our close call. He clapped Papa on the back. "You make a fine conductor. The Underground is lucky to have you."

As we followed the others into the barn, I thought, "But the Underground ain't got him no more, all 'cause of me." I wiped my eyes with the back of my hand and tried to picture us as a free family.

Inside the barn, Papa collapsed on a stool. "God watched over us." I suddenly understood that these runs weren't easy for Papa. Grams and Mama passed 'round tin plates of food, then Sam thanked Jesus for us all being together and alive. Plain beans and coffee never tasted so good.

Gramps, a short, dumpy man led our group to a horse stall. He kicked away the fresh straw and opened a trap door. "Hurry on down now!" He motioned for us to climb down the ladder to a small room under the barn floor. "Rest. Don't make no noise. Sun's up. My farm hands will be here soon to start the chores." I remembered Mama's words—"helping runaways escape is certain death, no matter the color of your skin." Gramps climbed down the ladder, behind the last of our group. "At dusk, we'll be moving on up to the next station. Stay quiet. Try to get some sleep."

After he and Grams were gone, I leaned against a wooden barrel in the dark room. I planned to be the lookout, but I fell asleep. In a blink, Mama shook me awake. "Grams needs our help. Follow me."

I stepped over sleeping folks and climbed the ladder up to the horse stall. The sunset was golden as Grams led Sam, Mama, Papa and me through the back door of their cozy clapboard house. She wiped her hands on her apron and looked close at Papa. "Oh, I recognize you now. You're the blacksmith from Dover Hall." Papa nodded. "When Gramps was moving the packages into the barn last night, I was busy cooking."

I frowned. "Packages? What packages?"

We followed her into a tidy kitchen. "That's what we call freedom seekers when they are being moved from station to station on the Underground," Grams said. She took a deep breath. "I could sure use some help bundling up the food. We're a bit behind schedule." She showed us how to tie biscuits, jerky, and carrots into red-checkered handkerchiefs. Papa and I fetched our sack of sweet 'tators from the wagon, and we added that to the food pile. Grams collected our food bundles and divided them into two laundry baskets. Then she covered them with clothes. "This is how I hide the food in case a slave catcher is nosing about. No one questions a woman with a laundry basket. Come along, now." Mama grabbed the other basket and we all slipped out the back door into the evening.

When we stepped inside the barn, Gramps was scooting crates and wooden barrels 'round on his flatbed wagon. He stopped and held up the lantern for a better look. "Grams? Is that you?"

"Yes, dear." Grams opened the trap door in the barn floor. "Come on out, folks. We got food. I'm sure you all are hungry now, but save some back in case the next station isn't safe and you have to keep going." The group climbed out and Mama and I handed out the bundles.

Papa and Sam went to help Gramps. The runaways gathered 'round Gramps' wagon waiting for his instructions. "I can take all of you in one trip if a couple ride in these empty barrels and a few of you in these crates." No one moved at first, but some of the younger folks spoke up since they could squeeze inside.

Papa and Sam helped the older folks lay down between the barrels and crates. Gramps covered up the folks and the crates and the barrels with empty feedsacks and travel blankets. Finally, piles of loose hay and supplies was put on top.

Just as I was getting settled into a hiding spot, Papa jumped down off the wagon. "Come over here, Peter." He pulled me over into a corner of the barn. Mama joined us. My stomach flip-flopped. Something didn't feel right 'bout this.

Chapter 19

Papa put his hands on my shoulders and looked me in the face. "Son, you knows we love you."

Goosebumps popped out on my arms. A bad feeling crawled all over me. I reached in my pocket for my Ogbe, but it was back at the cabin.

"Your Mama and I talked long and hard 'bout this 'fore deciding. We ain't going with you to Canada."

I couldn't breathe. It felt like Ratty Beard punched me in the gut, again. I fought to catch my breath and stammered, "Wha...what you saying? What 'bout us being a family in freedomland? If'n this is 'bout me causing trouble back at Dover Hall, I's sorry. I can make it up to you! But you cain't leave me. Please don't do this!"

Mama's tears looked like twin rivers down her face. "Son, we made a decision to risk our lives and others to save you from being sold down South. But we cain't turn our back on our Ibo promise made long 'fore we was sold into slavery."

"What...promise...you talking...'bout?" I was crying like a baby.

Papa hugged me hard. "E kwere m i me oke m: I agree to do my part. Our Underground work ain't done yet. We gots to help more of our kinsfolk. Our part is helping runaways be free. That's what the promise means."

Mama wrapped me in her arms, swaying.She whispered, "Massa Dover trusts us, and allows us more freedom than most. God blessed us with skills; me to sew the quilt codes and learn their meanings, and your Papa knows how to figure out the lay of the land. Creator gave us the tools we need to save our others. We was put here for this time and this place to lead our kinsmen to freedom." Mama stepped back and held me at arm's length. "Peter, never forget. One day we is coming back to you. Sam will look after you and teach you the carpentry trade 'till we can meet up with you in Canada. I love you, son." She let go of me and collasped into Gram's arms.

Papa held my face in his big, rough hands. "You 'member the crossroads we talked 'bout? We is at our family's crossroads now. We gots to choose which way we is going, the hard road or the easy road. Peter, your Mama and I is taking the hard road 'cause it leads to freedom for us and other enslaved folks. You is a man child now. You knows the quilt codes and how the Underground works. Even though it don't look like you 'll be a code keeper, like Mama and me, God has a plan for you. You go on ahead to Canada with Sam and start your life. When you is ready, you take up the Ibo promise to do your part. When I gots 'nough money to buy our freedom, we'll come find you. We love you, son. Never forget that."

As we walked back to Sam standing by the wagon, I clung to Papa like a wet blanket. "Let me come back with you. I can live in the woods or at a safe house close by. I can help you. Overseer John won't ever find me."

Gramps interrupted. "Time to go folks. I'll get you as close to the next station as possible, but we'll have to unload in the woods. Snake your way through the thicket towards the barn. Look for the lit lantern beside the door. That means it's safe. Once inside, climb up the ladder to the hayloft as fast as you can and hide under the loose hay."

Papa peeled my hands off his arm and Sam lifted me onto the wagon bed. "You gotta go, son. You'll never be safe anywhere near Dover long as Overseer John is breathing. God willing, we'll be together again one day."

Gramps clucked to the horses, and we rolled out of the barn. I sat like a rabbit frozen with fear. I couldn't believe this was happening. How could I live without my family? My last view was of Grams swaying back and forth with Mama in her arms. I could hear Mama's muffled sobs over the creaking wagon wheels. Papa stood staring at me. Tears soaked his shirt. The hurt was so deep, I thought I'd split in two.

I rolled up in a ball as the wagon traveled through the night. Sam laid a blanket over me. But I didn't care 'bout staying hid. I didn't care no more 'bout patrollers, or tracking dogs, or even Overseer John with his wicked whip. Nothing could hurt more than my heart being torn in half.

After what seemed like hours, Gramps pulled the horses to a stop in a grove of trees. "Here we are. Don't forget what I told you. Stay hidden in the hayloft until you hear a woman singing the hymn, Swing Low, Sweet Chariot. It will be Harriet, your next conductor. If you see her but she's not singing, don't come out! She's being watched. You wait. When she comes back singing, it'll be safe to come out of hiding. May God go with you."

Chapter 20

I lay in the wagon like a dead fish. Folks climbed around me and ran to the back of the barn. When no one was left but Sam, he took my arm. "Come on, Peter. We gotta hide. I'll help you, now. Like you helped me that day Overseer whipped me."

In the hayloft I cried and cried until I was wrung out like Mama's mopping rag. The days and nights blurred together as we stopped at safe house after safe house 'long the way. Sam kept telling me over and over that we was family now. We had to take care of each other. He never left my side.

The last stop on the Underground was the Cathedral Church in Canada. It had taken us two months to get there. Folks celebrated with dancing and singing. I paid no mind to what was happening 'round me. Our conductor told us we could own as much land as we could clear and plow.

Sam slapped me on the back. "We made it Peter! We is free!"

I is sure my smile must have looked as ugly as a jack-o-lantern's grin. Inside I was as empty as a hollowed out pumpkin. Sam scouted out a good piece of land, and we lived in a tent while we chopped down trees. It helped to keep my mind busy with building our cabin. My sadness never left but it faded a little each day.

When Sam talked 'bout how blessed we was to be free, 'cause of folks like Mama and Papa, I hid my face. I didn't want him to see my tears. Sam and I was starting a new life with no whips and no quotas and no separation of people 'cause of their skin color. I was getting to do what I had wanted for so long, be a carpenter. Sam and I began building cabins for others starting life as free people.

Years later, I was in town fetching supplies with Sam. I waited outside the general store for him to bring the wagon 'round so we could load up. Across the road I could see black and white children playing together. It reminded me of Em and me playing at Dover. A shadow crossed my path. I looked up, and just like she had jumped out of my thoughts, there stood Em.

Blonde curls shimmering in the sun, Em said, "As I live and breathe! Is that you Peter?"

I reached out to touch her, half expecting her to disappear in a puff of smoke. "Em? Emily Dover? Is you real?"

"Peter!" She grabbed me in a bear hug. "Course I'm real, you crazy boy. What are you doing here?"

"I live here now." I stepped back and noticed her mint green silk dress, matching gloves and parasol. "What is you doing here, Miss Em? Ain't you busy being the Missus of Dover Hall?" Then I panicked. "Is the Massa, uh, your Daddy with you?"

"Oh, no, Peter. Daddy passed last year." Those green eyes, I knew so well, sparkled with tears. "I have so much to tell you. Can you sit a spell?" She pulled me to the nearest bench, not waiting for my answer.

I took a deep breath. "Em, before you start jabbering, I got to know something. How's my Papa and Mama?"

"They're fine. But they miss you something terrible." She closed her parasol and took both my hands. "They work for me as mistress of Dover Hall. But not as slaves. I've given both of them their free papers, but your stubborn Papa insists on paying me his slave price of fifteen hundred dollars. Most of our former slaves took their papers and left right off. But some stayed on. They get a share of the profit from the harvest. We call them share-croppers. They can come and go as they please."

She could have knocked me over with a feather. "You kept your word 'bout not keeping slaves when you took over at Dover!" I hugged her. "I missed you, Em. I is so sorry I had to run, but I had no choice. Did Mama and Papa give you the note I left you?"

Em raised her eyebrows. "Your Mama gave me this tiny canoe." She held up my Ogbe. "When I missed you so much, I'd take it out of my pocket and stroke it because I knew you had carried it with you." She picked at her gloved hand. "No matter. I knew it was my fault you had to run. I was always getting you into trouble. I felt like you were the brother I never had. I was certain Daddy would see that and leave things be. I'm so sorry. Still friends?" She took off her glove and held out her pinky finger.

I grinned and hooked my pinky to hers. "Sure, Em. But not friends. We is family forever." Just then Sam pulled the wagon up to the front of the board walk. "Sam and I gots to load our supplies and get back to our cabin."

Em stood up. "I'm here to meet up with my husband, John. We are starting back home today. We just came to visit."

I hugged her one last time. "I 'member you always wanted to visit Canada."

A few years later, Mama and Papa did come find me in Canada. They told me what happened when they got back to Dover Hall. Our cabin had been ransacked. Overseer had come looking for me, just like we feared. When they cleaned up the broken furniture and dishes, Mama found my Ogbe stuck in the feather mattress. She kept it in her apron pocket, 'cause it made her feel close to me. Massa Dover questioned Mama and Papa 'bout my disappearance. He suspected they had helped me escape but he couldn't prove it. Overseer was itching to whip them, but Massa wouldn't let him. Instead, for a time, he took away Papa's extra work at other plantations and wouldn't let Mama help at the Butler Hospital.

One day Mama was taking Papa's lunch to him at the blacksmith shed, when Emily showed up. She sat on the grass watching Papa eat his lunch on the stump, like he always did. "I wanted to tell you how sorry I am for getting Peter in trouble." She picked blades of grass and threw them up in the air. It reminded Mama of when I'd sit at Papa's feet and do the same thing. "I loved Peter like a brother and am broken-hearted he is gone." Em covered her face and cried.

Mama walked over to her and pulled out my Ogbe from her apron pocket. "Miss Emily, Peter left this the night he disappeared. It is a piece of an Ibo canoe built by Papa when he was a boy in Africa. Papa breathed life giving words of protection over it and gave it to Peter on his tenth birthday. Peter carried it always. It has given me great comfort over these last months. But now I think on it, I believe he'd like for you to have it. To Peter, we was always just one big family. He could never see it any other way."

I never saw Em again, but I think of her from time to time. I wonder I she 'members me when she sees her kids playing with the hired-help at Dover Hall. Or maybe when she feels the tiny canoe in her pocket.

I smiled, knowing we had kept our pinky promises. We would be friends forever. No matter our skin color.

Plantation washing house

Enslaved children with wash pots

Public Sale of Negroes,

By RICHARD CLAGETT.

On Tuesday, March 5th, 1833 at 1:00 P. M. the following Slaves will be sold at Potters Mart, in Charleston, S. C.

Miscellaneous Lots of Negroes, mostly house servants, some for field work.

Conditions: ½ cash, balance by bond, bearing interest from date of sale. Payable in one to two years to be secured by a mortgage of the *Negroes*, and appraised personal security. *Auctioneer will pay for the papers.*

A valuable Negro woman, accustomed to all kinds of house work. Is a good plain cook, and excellent dairy maid, washes and irons. She has four children, one a girl about 13 years of age, another 7, a boy about 5, and an infant 11 months old. 2 of the children will be sold with mother, the others separately, if it best suits the purchaser.

Slave Sale Advertisement

Slave tag

Quilt Code Patterns

Basket: A triangular design shaped like a basket:
Code—Enslaved people were to pack their baskets with supplies, mostly food, because a group was planning to run soon.

Bear's Paw: A pattern using a square and five triangles arranged to look like a bear's paw print. It is believed it originated from the Native American slaves.
Code—They were to follow a bear's path, as it will lead you to caves for shelter, rivers for water, and honey and berries for food.

Bow Tie: Two triangles arranged to look like a man's bow tie.
Code—Runaways were to look for a hidden cache of nice clothes. They were to wash up, change into the nice clothes and walk through the nearby town pretending to be a free black person. This hid them in plain view.

Crossroads: A checkered pattern, representing an intersection in the routes to the north.
Code—Used when runaways had to make a decision whether to go towards Cleveland, Ohio or toward

Detroit, Michigan. Also represents when a person has to make a life-altering decision.

Drunkard's Path: A zig-zag pattern; In the Ibo tribes this design represented protection from evil spirits and was used in their shelters, clothing, jewelry, and even cut into their bodies.
Code—Runaways were to zig-zag through the woods to slow down the patrollers and make it more difficult for the dogs to track them.

Flying Geese: A series of triangle patterns.
Code—Tells runaways to follow the geese because they fly north in the spring, which is when most slaves escaped in order to avoid the cold weather.

Log Cabin: Starts with a square, then rectangle strips of fabric are added to build it out.
Code—It is generally believed the square must be a light color to represent a lantern in the window when it was safe house. A dark square in the middle was a warning to stay away, because the house was not a safe house.

Monkey Wrench: A respected caravan leader in the Ibo tribes of Africa, known for his navigation skills.
Code—In America's Antebellum South, this pattern indicated someone who would navigate runaways to a safe house on the Underground Railroad.

North Star: A star shaped pattern.
Code—Runaways were to look for the Big Dipper in the night sky and follow it to the North Star,

which would always lead them north. Slaves had no navigation tools to help them, only nature itself.

ShooFly: Shaped like a blacksmith's tool, it was a wood fan, shaped like a fancy carved canoe paddle mounted on the ceiling above the dining room table. It was connected to a rope pulley, used by a slave to keep flies and insects off the food.
Code—The pattern represented the enslaved man or boy who served the food and worked the fan during the meal. He was the only one allowed in the dining room while the family was present, so he overheard news, such as the calamitous Fugitive Slave Act.

Tumbling Blocks: A pattern that has a 3-D effect making it look like falling wooden blocks.
Code—It told enslaved people planning to run they needed to prepare, because a group would be leaving soon.

Wagon Wheel: A pattern representing a wagon wheel.
Code—Indicated there would be a wagon with a secret compartment to hide runaways that couldn't keep up, usually young children or the elderly.

Glossary

Bolls: The center part of the cotton plant that was picked. As the plant nears harvest it turns brown and woody with sharp edges.

Churndash: The paddles attached on a long stick inside a wooden barrel; used to stir cream into butter.

Clapboard: Long, thin, flat pieces of wood with edges horizontally overlapping in rows; used to cover the outside of houses.

Conductor/Monkey Wrench: A person who guided the runaways from safe house to safe house.

E kwere m jme oke m: Ibo tribal promise; "I agree to do my part."

Feedsack: A burlap bag used to carry feed for animals and food for people. Also used as blankets, and even clothing for the very poor.

Fugitive Slave Acts: A law Congress passed September 18, 1850 that required enslaved people be returned to their masters, even if they were living in a free state. The first Fugitive Slave Act was passed in 1793. It stated if enslaved people got to the northern, non-slave holding states above the Mason-Dixon line, they were considered free and could not be taken back to their owner.

Ibo/Iboland: (former spelling Igbo) One of three major ethnic groups in Nigeria, mostly on the eastern side of the Niger River located in the southeastern part of Africa.

Kinsmen: Your blood relations or tribe.

Lollygaggin': Being lazy, wasting time.

Mason-Dixon Line: The boundary existing between free states and slave states. It was the northern border of the slave-owning states before the abolition of slavery. Called freedomland by enslaved people.

Massa: The master, or owner, of the plantation and the enslaved people.

Midnight: Code name to refer to Detroit, Michigan, used by slaves planning to run.

North Star Station: A safe house owned by John Rankin up a hill across the Ohio-Kentucky River.

Ogbe: a talisman representing Ibo culture that has had a blessing of protection and life-giving powers spoken over it by elders/leaders of the tribe.

Passengers/packages: Runaways being moved between stations on the Underground Railroad by Conductors.

Patrollers: Organized groups of armed, mostly

white, men who hunted runaways for money during the Antebellum period. Sometimes called "pattyrollers" by enslaved people.

Praise House: The church where enslaved people were allowed to attend, and where Peter's Papa preached.

Quakers: A religious group that was against slavery. Many of these Abolitionists were Conductors on the Underground Railroad.

River Jordan: A river between Kentucky and Ohio, referencing the Jordan River in the Bible. Once the enslaved people crossed over into Ohio, they were free, according to the first 1793 Fugitive Slave Act.

Safe house/Stations: Safe places, usually houses with hidden cellars or secret rooms in an attic, where abolitionists hid slaves before moving them on to the next safe house—each getting them gradually closer to the North and freedom.

Skeeter time: Summer months, when mosquitoes carrying malaria were rampant. Plantation owners took their families north, or to Europe, during this time to protect them from the deadly diseases the mosquitoes carried.

Soiree/Gala: Elaborate party or ball.

Station Master: A conductor who lived at the safe house or station, and would take slaves on to the next station.

Surrey: A fancy carriage for two or four people, pulled by a horse or a team of horses.

Tator Bank: A cache dug in the ground to store sweet potatoes and potatoes. Looked like a small grave. The hole had to be deep enough to stay cool in the summer, and the layers of potatoes were separated by leaves so the potatoes would not rot.

Underground Railroad, or Underground: Originating in the slave states, a secret network of safe houses/stations scattered throughout the southern and northern states, leading all the way to Canada and Mexico. Slaves traveled secretly by all modes of hidden transportation between these houses as they made their way to freedom.

Whippersnapper: A smart mouthed trouble-maker.

Yoke: A wooden board worn behind the head and across the shoulders, with two buckets attached, one on each end, to carry water.

Author's Notes

This book is historical fiction. However, it is based on real, formerly enslaved people. Peter and Liza Farrow and their son, Peter Jr., lived on Thomas Dover's Plantation in Glen County, Georgia and used the secret Underground Railroad quilt codes which originated in the Kingdom of Benin (now Awka Nigeria).

Peter and Eliza and the UGRR network of abolitionists, risked their lives over and over to help many enslaved people reach freedom. Peter's metalsmith work was renown in the neighboring areas. Master Dover let him keep his earnings from outside jobs forging nails, gun parts, knives, the metal attachments for intricate staircase banisters, massive plantation gates and ornamental fences for surrounding plantations. Wherever his work took him, Peter preached, reaching out to enslaved people, and offering them hope and freedom. He became a respected "Monkey Wrench", also known as a Conductor, on the Underground Railroad. No one was ever captured under his watch.

Liza's coded quilt patterns based on Ibo/Adinkra cultural designs were passed down through the Farrow McDaniels, Strother families for five generations. It was a strict family secret until Peter's granddaughter, Ozella McDaniel Williams (Teresa R. Kemp's great aunt), explained the quilt codes to visitors to her quilt booth in the Charleston, South Carolina Slave Market. Women's History doctoral student, Jacqueline L. Tobin, returned several times to get more information to write Ozella's family story. She sought the help and expertise of Howard University's Dr. Raymond G. Dobard (Art History Professor) to reveal the UGRR quilt codes to the public in their book, Hidden in Plain View.

Peter and 'Liza Farrow literally lived out the Ibo proverb,

‘E kwere m i me oke m’. Translated, it means, I agree to do my part. As promised, Peter Sr. eventually earned enough money to buy their freedom in 1858, prior to the Civil War. They moved to Georgia and then South Carolina, where he continued working as a blacksmith and preaching the Gospel.

For more information go to:
https://ugrrquiltcode.blogspot.com/

Reverend Peter Farrow, Jr., born 1857

Bibliography

Browder, Anthony D., ASA Restoration Project: Youtube.com Wagon Wheel.

Cohen, Noam. "In Douglass Tribute, Slave Folklore and Fact Collide." New York: New York Times, 23 January 2007.

Ives, Sarah. "Did Quilts Hold Codes to the Underground Railroad?" National Geographic.com, 5 February 2004.

Kemp, Teresa R. Interviewed by author via text, phone and email, January 2018-2020.

Kemp, Teresa R. Keeper of the Fire: An Igbo Metalsmith of Awka. Amazon: CreateSpace, 2014.

Kemp, Teresa R. South Carolina's Wild's Heritage Center of Plantation Quilts website, summer, 2019.

Kemp, Teresa R. Interview, Joplin Missouri, January 4, 2020.

Raven, Margot Theis. Night Boat to Freedom. New York: Farrar, Straus and Giroux, 2006.

Tobin, Jacqueline, and Raymond Dobard. Hidden in Plain View: A Secret Story of Quilts and the Underground Railroad. New York: Random House, 1999.

Volckening, Bill. "Wonky World Blog Post". 19 September 2017.

Williams, Karen. Antebellum mansions' historic tour of Melrose Plantation, Natchez, Mississippi, April 2017.

For Further Reading:

Thomas- Joyce Jamey and Kemp, Teresa R. "Jamel's Deep-Sea Adventure", Createspace Charleston SC 2015.

Davies Nicola "Exploring the Oldest Fabrics in Existence".https://aatcc.org/exploring-the-oldest-fabrics-in-existence/ , AATCC Newsletter 20 March 31, 2020..

Author, KJ Williams

KJ Williams loves connecting kids to books. She spent thirty-seven years as a schoolteacher and media specialist encouraging children to discover books and love reading. Williams ignited their imagination with her debut book, **Camp Not Allowed**.

Keepers of the Secret Code came to life as Williams watched her mother sew quilts with the coded patterns. This story of ingenuity, unity, persistence and fighting for freedom at all costs haunted her. When she met Teresa R. Kemp, whose family had kept the secret quilt code for generations, KJ knew she had to write it down and share this incredible story with children across all cultures.

Follow KJ's writing journey at: www.booklover1.com.

Co-Author, Teresa R. Kemp

Kemp was born in Germany and graduated from Berlin American High School. At 15 years of age she flew to America to attend Ohio State University. She transferred to West Virginia State College (now WVSU) outside of Charleston, West Virginia, where she majored in Political Science and History.

Ten years later, Teresa moved to Atlanta, Georgia and married Calvin Kemp, Jr. She returned to school and graduated from DeVry University with a Bachelor of Science degree in Computer Information Systems.

Kemp is the great-granddaughter of a plantation owner and a Native American. Her ancestors include Reverend Peter and Eliza Farrow, slaves on the Dover Hall plantation in Glynn County, Georgia. The Farrows used, and passed down, the secret quilt codes to assist the Underground Railroad.

Teresa has twelve grandchildren and five great-grand children. In 2005, Teresa along with her parents opened the Ungerground Railroad Quilt Code Museum in Underground Atlanta, GA. Teresa's books and presentations continue to preserve her family's richly diverse legacy.

Meet the Authors

Teresa R. Kemp & KJ Williams

Notes

CPSIA information can be obtained
at www.ICGtesting.com
Printed in the USA
LVHW012055220921
698519LV00004B/61